"I said freeze  **gh gritted teeth**

She tried to catch up as the man darted into the adjoining room where Joe held someone's hands behind their back with one hand.

"Joe," she called out. He looked up in time to see the man running his way. He whirled around, but the man struck Joe's head with the flashlight. Joe groaned and dropped to the ground.

The man and his freed accomplice wasted no time running to the door. Kendra raised her weapon and aimed at the set of fluorescent lights. She pulled the trigger and a heartbeat later the glass rained down, but the two figures rushed past the door and disappeared. Kendra ran forward.

"Joe?" She touched his face. He was unconscious. Sometimes an impact to the head could be so intense the brain actually hits against the skull and shuts down, hopefully only for a moment.

She slid her fingers to the spot underneath his chin and lightened the pressure. *Please let me find his heartbeat.*

Heather Woodhaven earned her pilot's license, rode a hot-air balloon over the safari lands of Kenya, parasailed over Caribbean seas, lived through an accidental detour onto a black-diamond ski trail in Aspen, and snorkeled among stingrays before becoming a mother of three and wife of one. She channels her love for adventure into writing characters who find themselves in extraordinary circumstances.

Books by Heather Woodhaven

Love Inspired Suspense

Twins Separated at Birth

Undercover Twin
Covert Christmas Twin

Calculated Risk
Surviving the Storm
Code of Silence
Countdown
Texas Takedown
Tracking Secrets
Credible Threat
Protected Secrets

COVERT
CHRISTMAS
TWIN

HEATHER
WOODHAVEN

◆ HARLEQUIN® LOVE INSPIRED® SUSPENSE

Recycling programs
for this product may
not exist in your area.

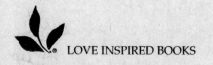 LOVE INSPIRED BOOKS

ISBN-13: 978-1-335-23240-3

Covert Christmas Twin

www.Harlequin.com

Printed in U.S.A.

In all thy ways acknowledge him,
and he shall direct thy paths.
–Proverbs 3:6

To my readers—
I hope you don't eat as many Christmas goodies
while reading as I did while writing this.
Though, if you want my recommendation,
gingerbread men are the way to go.

ONE

Kendra Parker reached the entrance to the lecture hall and listened to the voice reverberating through the door. She'd heard somewhere that a child would always recognize their mother's voice, but what if she'd never heard it before? What if her birth mother had handed over Kendra and her twin to someone without a word? This professor's voice rang strong, without much emotion, as she rattled off some historic study on behavior analysis. Kendra couldn't detect anything in her voice alone.

Her phone felt heavy in her pocket as she itched to text Audrey, the newfound twin she'd discovered in the midst of an FBI operation gone wrong. In fact, the mission had gone so wrong, Kendra had been shot and her partner, Special Agent Lee Benson, felt it necessary for Audrey to take Kendra's place in the deep-cover assignment. It'd been six weeks since Kendra had seen her sister return to normal life, with the odd exception of Lee's plans to marry Audrey soon.

Kendra had used the last six weeks to track down leads in an effort to locate their mother, but now she hesitated. She left the phone untouched since it could turn out to be another dead end, and her twin was a lot more sensitive—despite being a genius PhD at Caltech—to disappointment. Instead, Kendra needed to treat this like any other FBI assignment and stifle her emotions to get the job done. No more stalling.

She hauled open the door to find the classroom set up like a theater. Only a few students gave her half glances before they returned to their laptops, typing away notes as Professor Beverly Walsh lectured without missing a beat. Kendra lowered herself into a chair five rows down, in the first open aisle seat to her left, but unlike the students, she had no interest in lifting the retractable desktop. Her interest was solely in the professor with straight blond hair—first strike, as both Kendra and Audrey had curly brown hair. The professor's face, though, was turned away as she wrote on the blackboard:

Cluster of cues for deceit: hand touching, face touching, crossing arms, leaning away.

Kendra's neck heated with the instinctive knowledge that someone was studying her. She turned around as if to examine her armrest, but surveyed the students in the seats around her. No one seemed to be paying her any attention.

"Together, as a cluster, these cues—" the professor tapped on the board with the chalk "—indicate deceit. Separately, they mean nothing, unless…" The professor turned. "Anyone?" Approximately in her fifties, the woman was short in stature—second strike—and shorter than Kendra, who stood a little over five foot seven. The brown pants, buttoned, burgundy cardigan and light blue scarf looked classy—third strike—and professional. Kendra didn't recognize her own style on the professor at all.

Professor Walsh pointed at a man in the front row. The student casually lowered his hand and leaned forward. "Single cues of deceit can be accurate if a previously collected baseline indicates such." His voice resonated with a deep and soothing timbre.

From Kendra's diagonal viewpoint, he appeared to be in his early thirties and had thick dark hair, carefully styled, and a relaxed posture that didn't match the crisp, blue-collared shirt peeking out from the black canvas jacket. She couldn't shake the feeling that she should know who the man was, but she couldn't quite place him. If he turned another fifteen degrees, she'd be able to get a better look at his face.

The professor nodded as she stepped back and regarded the rest of the class. Her green eyes passed over Kendra, and both her posture and face stiffened, as if the professor had just smelled something distasteful. She settled into a neutral face a heartbeat later.

Kendra's stomach churned. She didn't know how, and couldn't claim to be a behavioral analyst, but every fiber of her being felt that Beverly Walsh had recognized her. If Kendra hadn't been watching, she very well would've missed it. Her mouth turned dry. She'd found her mother.

"That's probably enough for today, so I'll end class a bit early," the professor said. "Consider it extra study time for your exam on Friday." She grabbed the books and papers resting on the top of a podium and stuffed them into a leather messenger bag, then slipped out of a side door next to the blackboard.

Students rushed toward the aisle, filling the stairway leading to the public exit at the top. Kendra dodged them, fighting the stream. To her left, the student who had prompted the professor's smile stepped down from the first row.

Kendra held back a gasp as their eyes met. She recognized the olive skin, the eyes that matched a stormy sky and the soft smile that suddenly disappeared. His name escaped her, but she knew him. There was no time for a reunion to figure out where, though. She darted across the classroom floor and out the door.

A musty hallway lit by only three fluorescent lights assaulted her sinuses and provoked the start of a tension headache. At the far end, Beverly Walsh hustled toward the exit door. "Professor," Kendra called. She couldn't yell out "Mom" yet. That would be too weird.

Beverly shoved the crash bar and as the door swung open, bright sunshine flooded the hallway. Then she disappeared from sight. Kendra hesitated for the briefest of seconds, second-guessing her instincts. Logically, how would Beverly know Kendra was her daughter if she hadn't seen her since birth? Maybe there was another reason she was running away that didn't have anything to do with adoption.

Kendra bolted forward, pumping her arms, until she burst out the door a few seconds after the professor. She squinted against the sunshine. The Florida campus was dotted with trees so thick it would be easy to hide. She didn't spot any students so it seemed to be a rarely used exit, although it was the first Monday morning after Thanksgiving, a prime skip day.

Strands of blond hair swung out from behind a tree. The professor's swinging hair had given away her location. Even if this woman wasn't her mother, Kendra wasn't used to people running away from her unless they had something to hide. She broke into a jog, and with long strides, gained on the professor.

"Get down!" a man's voice yelled from behind.

A shot rang out from above. Bark chipped off the tree and flew into her face. Kendra held up both arms to block the flying bits of wood from hitting her eyes. She dropped to the ground, rolling behind a tree.

She popped up on one knee, facing the direction of the shot, and reached behind to pull out her own gun. The sun made it difficult to see clearly, but she spotted the shadow of a man in an open window on the top floor. A glint of reflection, most likely a scope, pointed her way.

She raised her weapon and aimed. Another bullet sounded before she could pull the trigger. She flinched, remembering all too well what it felt like for a bullet to pierce her flesh. This time, the pain never came.

The man dropped from the open window. Kendra hadn't shot him, hadn't had a chance to fire. She whipped her head around to prevent seeing the gunman hit the pavement, only to find the man she'd recognized in class putting away his weapon. His military stance helped the name rush to the forefront of her mind—Joe Rose, FBI behavioral analyst unit officer.

The professor appeared in her periphery, then rushed past her, toward the broken body on the ground. She bent over and searched his pockets until she pulled out the man's phone. She pocketed it and rushed toward Kendra while beckoning Joe with her index finger. "Well, this is a fine mess you've gotten us into."

Her green eyes flashed as she met Kendra's gaze. "Put away your weapon! You've already caused enough trouble walking into my class without warning. Would you like a sign that says, 'Please kill me'?"

Beverly walked a few more steps, her gait short but unbelievably fast as she rounded another tree. She spun around. "We need to get out of sight now. This place is about to explode with people and law enforcement."

Kendra blinked, a flood of hurt and confusion threatening to slow her down, but she rushed after Beverly as if on autopilot. Joe reached her side and pointed at a building up ahead, past another set of trees. She wanted to ask him a million questions but held her tongue. Nothing made sense. She didn't understand enough about what had just happened to even form an educated question. They rounded another building just as sirens reached their ears.

"Someone found the body already. Great." Beverly shook her head. "We're on borrowed time, then. Would it have killed you to use a silencer, Joe?"

"It may surprise you to find out I don't carry one, Beverly. I thought it'd be best to save Special Agent Parker's life instead." His voice remained calm and collected despite the professor's irritated tone. He turned to Kendra and smirked as if the expression could be a form of greeting. "I'm hoping to find out why she's here."

"I assume Kendra's figured out I'm her mother. She practically waved a banner back there informing everyone else, too." Her eyes flashed but only glanced at Kendra for half a second. "Let's hope you haven't already put a target on your head."

Kendra kept up the pace but felt like she'd entered some alternate universe. She shook her head and stopped abruptly. "Excuse me. Did I miss a memo? Did I black out and not hear, I don't know, how you know who I am?" She bit out the last few words.

Beverly sighed, disappointment drenching her every feature. "Let's get somewhere secure and then I'll brief you."

"Brief me?" Except Beverly had already taken off, booking it so fast she was out of earshot. Kendra turned to Joe. "Is my mo—" She almost choked on the word *mother*. Her brain refused to digest that she'd actually found her after all this time. Or, perhaps Kendra wasn't sure the woman deserved the title. "Is Beverly Walsh a Fed?"

Joe shrugged, a sympathetic smile on his face. He reached for her hand and led her after the speed-walking Beverly. "I'm afraid it's a little more complicated than that."

In any other scenario, Joe Rose would've wanted to take Kendra to a coffee shop and properly catch up on their lives. But, seeing as he'd just shot a man who had tried to kill her, it was probably best to take Beverly's lead and keep moving.

It'd been years since he'd last seen Kendra, back in their training days at the FBI Academy. Work Hard, Play Hard seemed to be her motto back then. If his analysis proved correct, it stemmed partly from an inner drive Joe couldn't relate to and a fierce desire to prove something. To whom, he didn't know.

The years—or perhaps the job—had taken an obvious toll on her. She looked the same—it wasn't that—but her eyes reflected a deep weariness as well as a guarded nature he didn't remember being there before. She looked leaner, stronger physically, yet more vulnerable. Perhaps he'd spent too much time studying lately and was reading too much into her appearance. She had, after all, just met her birth mother and narrowly avoided being killed.

Kendra tugged slightly on his hand, and only then did he realize he was still holding hers. He silently prayed for wisdom and protection, then gave her fingers a light squeeze and let go. Beverly's speed walk could beat many runners, but she turned—a good twenty paces ahead of them—and made the universal symbol for "stop" with her hand. Joe slowed, no longer attempting to catch up. She gave him a nod of approval and disappeared around a corner. He felt certain he knew where she was headed.

"I appreciate the help, but you're not my analyst and this isn't a mission, so you don't need to lead me by the hand," Kendra said. "In fact, I don't really understand why you're here, so I hope you'll explain that, as well."

"Of course." He shrugged. "It wasn't intentional. I'm a pastor now. I mean, I'm transitioning to become one full-time. I'm taking steps to leave the Bureau, at least." He cringed, trying to figure out how to back up and explain better.

She halted. "What?" Her gaze darted ahead, and she

seemed to notice that Beverly had disappeared from their line of vision. "Great. I'm losing her."

"Beverly wanted us to split up. There could be eyes watching her." Joe stepped into a side alley. "I think she's going to her place, her real place. She has a town house for show, but I've been to her actual house once. It's probably best we go a different way to meet her."

"I have a million questions that won't wait and—" She placed her hands on her hips and regarded him. "Why do I have the feeling you already know what I'm going to ask?"

He took a deep breath. It felt like lying not to admit what he knew. "I found out recently about you and your twin sister, Audrey. The circumstances for you meeting Beverly today aren't ideal, but—"

She took a step backward and bit her lip before a mask of nonchalance dropped in place. "*How* did you find out I have a twin? I didn't even know until a few months ago, and ever since then, the FBI has been diligent in making sure no one else found out. So I know whatever you're doing here with my—with Beverly—isn't FBI-sanctioned. Why are you here, Joe?"

His recent training taught him how to handle many a delicate moment, but this discussion felt like entering an unmarked minefield. He exhaled, trying and failing to imagine what meeting Beverly had to be like for her. "You should know that even though Beverly seems like a hard woman, I know for a fact she cares more than she'd ever admit. Beyond that, answering your question right now is a little tricky. I'm not sure it's my place to really—"

She grabbed his shoulder and turned him until they

were face-to-face. "It's about me, Joe. I think it's my place to know. Start talking." Her cheeks reddened slightly and she let go and took a step back. "Please. It's not a pleasant sensation to feel like you're the last to know who your own mother is."

He studied her face, missing the smile that had been on her face so often back at Quantico. "Like I was trying to tell you, I'm actually in the process of resigning from the Bureau. I took an extended leave that's about to be permanent."

Her eyebrows rose. "Why? You have a great reputation."

"That's nice to hear, but I found it just wasn't for me. I came here to utilize the theology—"

Kendra placed a hand on her hip. "Joe, how many degrees do you have now?"

He collected degrees like most people did books, although he mostly stuck to the fields of psychology and sociology. "Only five. I've been auditing your mo—" He caught himself before saying mother. "Beverly's classes. Actually, she was the one who made me realize I wasn't ready to completely cut ties with the FBI. So after I tender my resignation, I'll apply to continue with the FBI on a volunteer basis."

"Volunteer? You can't volunteer for the FBI."

"As an FBI chaplain."

She pulled her chin back and frowned. "Huh?" The sirens grew louder as the sound of revving motors got closer. She pointed to his arm. "Walk with me."

He did as she asked. She grabbed his hand with her right and walked with him, head down, as if they were a couple strolling. "Until I know what's going on, I think it's best to leave the police out of the loop. Look up and act surprised by what's happening."

Three police cars zoomed past them. The air crackled with the chaos that came after a shooting. Joe wasn't ready to process that he'd been the one to fire a bullet that had taken a life, even if he only did it to save a life.

Another cruiser slowed ever so briefly as the officer in the passenger side glanced at them. They were looking for the shooter, but Kendra's face showed the perfect amount of confusion and concern that he knew the officer would assume they were just bystanders. His suspicion was confirmed as the officer shook his head and they zoomed away, likely to check all the nearby alleys.

"Covert work comes naturally to you, doesn't it?" He couldn't help but wonder if she pretended to be part of a couple with a lot of agents.

Kendra dropped his hand. "I don't mean to be rude, but can you get to the part about my supposed mother telling you about me?"

Another reminder it wasn't time to catch up. "Yes. She's made brilliant discoveries in the field of behavior analysis, she's an excellent professor and—" he peeked around the brick building before rounding the corner "she's also watched very closely by hired guns, like the one who tried to kill you."

He pointed ahead to a blue Victorian house that from the outside appeared to be falling apart. The porch sagged and the landscaping, while trimmed neatly, contained more weeds than grass. Even the windows were covered in grime from years of neglect. They would have to cross the street, in the open, to reach it. "I really think I should let her have a chance to explain the rest. You won't have to wait much longer."

The time he'd spent with Beverly taught him she was a woman so defined by pain she couldn't see life as offering anything else. He needed to weigh his words with care and make sure he didn't interfere with any chance for her and Kendra to make amends. "If you have any questions afterward, I'll be glad to tell you what I know."

She exhaled, her curled lip expressing her distaste for his decision.

"I promise," he added. The compulsion to say such a thing surprised him.

A silver sedan turned the corner. He gestured for Kendra to step in the shadow made by a nearby dumpster, and they pressed their backs against the brick until it passed. "Oh, and, Kendra?"

Her wide green eyes studied him. "Yes?"

"If she thinks you're in danger, you have every reason to believe her."

TWO

Kendra followed Joe through the side door of the Victorian house. The place appeared to be standing on its last legs. Inside was no better. Dust swirled in the sunbeams shining through the front windows. The wooden floors were warped from age and possible flooding, and the furniture sported beige tarps. "You're telling me *this* is where Beverly really lives?"

She hadn't needed Joe to tell her about the other house Beverly apparently kept for show. Kendra had already looked it up online. Why anyone would choose to actually live in an old dump over a home with modern upgrades, though, was beyond her.

Joe walked down the hallway, stopped at a metal basement door and knocked to the musical rhythm of "Shave and a Haircut."

"Really?"

He flashed what she considered to be his trademark smirk, the one she'd felt drawn to during their time at the academy. He had to know how attractive he looked wearing that mischievous expression. The sound of metal sliding echoed around them. Joe turned the handle and swung open the door to reveal carpeted stairs and an electronic lock and keypad installed on the wall.

She fought to keep her face neutral, knowing he was watching for her reaction. He closed the door behind her and pressed the red lock button on the keypad. They descended into an apartment complete with gleaming wooden floors, stainless kitchen appliances, lighting that mimicked natural sunlight and colorful red and blue love seats arranged around a tiled coffee table covered in hardback books.

Beverly stepped out of a side room to face them, her blond hair pulled into a ponytail. She'd already changed into jeans and a hunter green sweater. She crossed her arms across her chest. "How'd you find out?"

Kendra clenched her jaw. The nerve. If anyone deserved answers, it was her. Fine, she'd play Beverly's game, but only because Joe had promised to tell all later. "I chased down every informant and asset I've ever had. After a little pushing, I found a common thread in about a third of my cases. Anonymous tips that seemed too convenient, some in the form of emails, some texts. I called in some unofficial favors to track—"

"And likely caused a lot of attention." Beverly glanced at Joe and flicked her wrist. "Those tips weren't convenient at all. I was trying to help keep you safe, which you've just thrown away."

Kendra thought she'd been prepared for her first conversation with her birth mother. She'd imagined it countless times while trying to set up shields around her heart, and yet, this wasn't matching any of the planned scenarios. Her throat tightened as she breathed deeply and tried to get control over her emotions. Beverly's words alone indicated she cared, but her tone threatened to break Kendra.

Beverly held up the phone she'd taken off the dead man's body and shoved the screen in Kendra's direction. "You're officially a target."

I recognize a Fed. Clearly not a student.

The response below read: Keep me apprised.

Kendra remembered feeling like she was being watched in the classroom, but no one had raised a red flag before the attempted shooting. She glanced up. "I wasn't the only Fed. This text could mean Joe."

Beverly shook her head. "No. They know he's quitting to become a pastor. I made sure of it before he audited my class. There's no security cameras on that side of the building, but if he was spotted shooting—" She inhaled, shook her head and reached to scroll down the screen to the next text.

Prof is running away from Fed now.

The response sent a chill down Kendra's spine. Take Fed out.

Her mother grabbed the phone back from her, flipped it over and removed the battery. "It's only a matter of time until they realize he didn't succeed." She shoved both parts of the phone into a black mesh bag that, judging by the symbols, looked to be the type to block a tracking signal.

"That doesn't explain why a gunman was watching

you." Kendra's hackles rose. "You said you would brief me. That usually includes more than vague pronouns."

Beverly pulled back her shoulders and pursed her lips, a movement Kendra recognized as the expression she also flashed when annoyed. An odd feeling of connection rose and fell like a wave.

"The owner of this phone was part of the illegal group known as Masked—you should recognize the name since they've been a top FBI priority—and whoever sent this text is especially edgy after the loss of their secure communications."

Kendra frowned. "Masked was a cellular network designed solely for organized crime use, but the FBI completely dismantled it." Actually, it was the mission where her twin had taken over for her, so, technically, Audrey had helped to dismantle Masked, but Beverly didn't need to know the details. She glanced at Joe. "The FBI issued a press release weeks ago once they were sure they got everyone. The Masked Network is no more."

"*Network* is the key word." Beverly held up a finger. "You only got their communications. The actual goal of Masked is to recruit agents, soldiers, intelligence and technologies of value to sell to the highest bidder, usually foreign entities. Masked is the brainchild of one person, and I think that person, a man who refers to himself as the Pirate, is a mole within one of our federal agencies."

The news felt like a slap in the face. Surely, Beverly didn't know what she was talking about. "If what you are saying is true, why didn't all the people the FBI arrested rat him out?"

"Two reasons. By design, members only know those within their own segment of the organization. I'm sure they've never met the Pirate since he's the world's safest delegator. Well, until recently, after you and your partner took down communications."

Kendra crossed her arms, unnerved by Beverly's last statement. "I never said anything about my partner or I being involved." In fact, only a select group at the FBI knew that information, and only a few knew that Audrey had taken her place. "I think it's time you tell me how you know about this pirate."

"Because the Pirate recruited me." Beverly sank down onto the armrest of the closest couch. "I put myself in a position to be snatched up by Masked. My deep-cover assignment is to get into the inner circle and identify the Pirate. I've worked my way up to head analyst, but have yet to meet him."

"Deep cover for what agency?"

For a moment it seemed Beverly would refuse to answer, then she sighed. "I report only to the director of NCS."

"You're NCS?" Kendra didn't bother keeping the surprise from her voice. The National Clandestine Service, the little-known undercover arm of the CIA, served as the primary source of human intelligence in the nation. The NCS operated differently than any other federal agency. Rumored to skip written reports, they were so secret that even the director of the division wasn't officially disclosed. "Do you think the Pirate works in your division?" The idea seemed logical, as the NCS served as the national authority for all evaluation of undercover operations across the intelligence community.

Beverly offered a half-hearted shrug. "Initially. But, if that was the case, I don't believe the FBI would've succeeded in taking down their communication network, which funded much of their recruiting efforts. And, ever since that takedown, all integral members of Masked have been carefully watched."

"That's why you have a gunman following you around?"

"Yes. The organization is wounded and suspicious, but the last thing we want is for them to go underground and rebuild." Another phone buzzed and Beverly glanced at it. "Masked wants a status report from me about the Fed."

"Maybe you can stall them," Kendra offered. "Text a mission-complete status."

"Won't do any good. The body has already been found. That man wasn't the only one that kept tabs on me. They rotate shifts."

Another buzz. Beverly shook her head. "Great. Now Masked wants me to check in, physically." She stood. "I need to stay on their good side and stall them. There weren't any security cameras on that side of the building, but it's only a matter of time until they realize who you are. As soon as they figure out you and your partner broke up their communications network, they'll want all of us dead. Joe, I'm afraid that includes you. I figure we only have one shot to take them down, or we'll need to go underground, permanently."

"WITSEC?" Joe asked.

"You can't get witness protection if you don't know whom you need protection from." She turned to Kendra. "Can I dare hope you've secured your sister's research?"

Kendra caught herself pulling back her shoulders and pursing her lips, then realized what she was doing and shook her head instead. "What are you talking about?"

Beverly threw up her hands. "I thought it was obvious. I arranged for you to meet your sister. I sent Audrey's last-minute invite to the conference at Stanford. I had a tip you'd be there."

The blood felt like it'd left Kendra's face. "You arranged for us to meet?"

"Of course. There's no time to explain it all, Kendra. The point is your sister's research is very important. I thought for sure you'd connect the dots by now."

She wanted to open her mouth and tell Beverly that she couldn't play with people's lives like that—

"Audrey is on the cusp of a breakthrough in the advancement of metamaterials."

Joe whistled low. "Are we talking cloaking technology? Is she working on upgrades to what the military is using?"

Kendra wanted to roll her eyes at his enthusiasm. Yes, her sister was a genius, big-shot government grant researcher at Caltech. "I don't know. Maybe."

"I've been hearing murmurs that the Pirate is going after Audrey's research."

Kendra's neck tingled. "Are you saying she's in danger?"

Beverly hesitated before she shook her head. "I don't believe so. He has no interest in recruiting her personally and won't want to draw attention. He only wants to obtain and sell the research." Her phone vibrated again, and she began rushing around the room, gathering items and shoving them in a duffel bag. "He usually asks me to analyze someone for the best way to bribe them, but in this scenario, he said he already knew how to obtain what he wanted."

"You're saying the Pirate already knows someone at the lab will hand over the research."

"Yes. Either he's already commissioned someone to infiltrate the lab, or, I believe, based on his behavior, that he's planning to infiltrate the lab himself. It's in the best interests of our national security that he doesn't succeed. If he sold it to another country—" Beverly reached a hand out to put on her shoulder but Kendra instinctively took a step backward. "This is probably the only chance to get our hands on the Pirate. You've met your sister now. Do you think you could take her place?"

A regular twin swap, just like when Audrey had taken her place on the mission. Only this time it would be Kendra's turn to pretend she was Audrey. She'd probably have jumped at the idea if she'd been in high school, but now, the request infuriated her. "I'm sure it would've been easier had I grown up knowing her."

"We don't have time for this!" Beverly's eyes blazed. "You want to know why you didn't? Your father was a double agent. Does that make you feel better?" Beverly blinked rapidly. "Obviously, I didn't know that when I married him," she said in a softer voice. "Seven months pregnant, I intercepted a message that as soon as you were born, his orders were to kill me and kidnap you and your sister. I ran away, had you two and gave you up for adoption to keep you safe. Because what kind of life could I give you, constantly running away from a double agent?" Her voice wobbled as she raised her chin. "Months later, I knew I made the right decision when he found me."

Joe stepped forward. "Okay, maybe we should wait to unpack history until—"

Kendra ignored him. She couldn't take a break from hearing the whole story. This was the reason she'd tracked down Beverly in the first place—to find out the whole truth. Her heart beat so fast she could hardly think straight. "Is he still alive?"

Beverly turned away. "It was either him or me." Her phone buzzed a third time. "Does the FBI know you're here?"

Kendra fought to focus on her question when all her mind wanted to do was play the news about her parents on a loop. "No. All the FBI knows is I took a leave of absence."

Beverly exhaled. "Well, that's something. It'll make it harder for Masked to figure out which Fed was here, but we still don't have much time. Go. Take Audrey's place in the lab. Secure the research and figure out the Pirate's identity before anyone in Masked discovers Special Agent Parker is my daughter. Joe, go with her—"

"I'm not so sure—"

Beverly leveled a harsh stare at him. "She can't trust anyone else. She needs backup and a good analyst to help her. It's why I've been training you."

He blinked rapidly, and they both turned to Beverly at the same time. Joe's mouth dropped. "What?"

Joe held up his hands. "What do you mean 'training' me?" He replayed every discussion he could remember with Beverly from the past six weeks. "You came to the church after service one day and told me you were having a crisis of faith. You said you thought your classes would be useful to my ministry because—"

"Ever since Kendra shut down the network, the Pirate has become a little neurotic with trust issues," Beverly said.

"You call it trust issues. I call it fear of being arrested," Kendra said.

Joe shook his head. "She's trying to say I've been the middle man for her reports to the director of the NCS. I've delivered some flash drives to a dead drop at the hospital when I'm making my visiting rounds. It's why she read me in about her undercover work with NCS." But he never thought she was trying to train him for anything. She did offer him a lot of extra tutelage in her behavior analysis classes, but he thought she was simply passionate about the field of study.

Beverly shook her head. "That's not why I read you in, Joe. I told you about Kendra and Audrey because you were useful as an asset, not because I was having a crisis of faith."

The way Beverly said the last three words made him wonder if she'd ever believed or if she'd used his faith as a way to manipulate him into doing what she wanted.

"I was aware of your analyst background and that you already knew Kendra," she continued. "It was a long shot that Kendra would secure Audrey's research without a mandate, although I hoped. I was preparing you as an asset to go help her. My class curriculum was geared toward what you'd need to know to stand up against Masked."

She'd only wanted to train him for a mission? Was that the real reason she'd wanted him in her classes? "And what if I say no?" He wasn't a puppet.

She crossed her arms and leaned back, a sure sign Beverly knew she had the upper hand. "Do I have to remind you who shot that man today? You have the freedom to say no, but you'd be putting your own life, that of your congregants, Kendra and I, and anyone else who gets near you, in danger if the Pirate isn't stopped."

Joe's stomach flipped. He hated the thought of taking a life, but he'd only done so to spare Kendra. Beverly knew as much. She was, after all, the expert in behavior analysis. She knew he wouldn't stand for putting anyone in danger if he could help it.

Beverly nodded, as if she saw the agreement on his face before he'd felt it. "Don't trust anyone else in the FBI or any of the other law-enforcement agencies. There are ears everywhere. I have to disappear now. Please, do what I ask. If you fail, we'll never get to finish this conversation."

"Because we'll all be dead. Yes, we get the picture," Joe stated.

A beeping sounded from across the room. Beverly spun and walked to the computer against the wall and clicked on the monitor. "I apparently didn't remove the gunman's phone battery fast enough. They've already tracked it to here." She groaned. "I'm getting too old for this."

"Are you sure they haven't been tracking your phone?" Kendra asked.

Beverly's smile could only be described as condescending. She reached underneath the desk and pulled out a stuffed backpack. A hat and glasses were tossed Kendra's way. "Put those on and get out of here. I'm assuming you have some covers prepared. Use them. Do you your best to keep your identity hidden." She handed Joe a hat, along with a pack of three driver's licenses, all with his photograph and fake names on them and a stack of Visa gift cards.

He stared at his image. "You really have been preparing to send me."

"Keep her safe, Joe."

"I'll do my best." Despite the gnawing feeling that he'd been handled, he knew the right thing to do was help Kendra.

"With all due respect, I'm the special agent. I'm pretty sure I'll be keeping *him* safe," Kendra snapped. Her cheeks flushed as if she'd just realized she'd spoken aloud.

"I'll let you two recount who saved who," Beverly said. The monitor beeped again. Two cars on two different camera angles appeared on the screen. "Take the back exit now."

"What about you?" Kendra asked, her voice rising.

"Worry about yourself. They're coming. Go!"

THREE

Never before had Kendra felt so belittled and confused, and that was saying something since she'd been through the FBI Academy. No time for logical explanations or discussions. No, of course not. Instead, one interaction with her spy birth mother, and Kendra found herself running for her life.

She followed Joe, as he ascended the stairs by only taking every other step, since he knew the house layout best. He waited for her at the top before opening the door. "As long as it's still clear, we head for the back door. There are bushes on each side—not a good safety feature for a normal person—"

"Joe, there's no time to be analyzing the security for—"

"Right. Our visitors will probably be drawn to the front and side entrances. As long as they're not at the back yet, we make a run for the neighbor's house. It's empty. I noticed the foreclosure sign when we approached. You can pick a lock, right?"

"Yes, but I don't always carry a lock-picking set."

He raised an eyebrow as if in disbelief.

"Fine. I brought one with me today, but I really don't carry it at all times." Truth was, if she hadn't interacted with the professor at the classroom, she'd planned to investigate the town house before leaving. Not exactly legal, but she'd justified the possibility since she had potential evidence that her birth mother was tampering with her federal investigations by providing anonymous tips. Now, there was no need. Beverly had admitted as much.

"Unlock the back for us next door, and we can hide in there until the coast is clear enough to make it to my car."

Kendra was used to calling the shots when working with a partner, but Joe seemed ready to take the reins. Showing her the way out of the house was one thing, but planning out the mission was another. "My rental car makes more sense. We can ditch it before there's any need to track it, and I didn't use my real name to rent it. If it stays at the college campus it'll draw attention, especially given the shooting investigation, and lead to my identity being discovered faster."

Beverly poked her head around the bottom of the staircase. "Go already. The back is clear!"

"I forgot she had cameras there, too." Joe pressed the open button on the keypad and they burst through the door, down a long hallway lined with tall windows covered in green roller shades, through a kitchen that still held a woodstove and old-fashioned refrigerator. If they had the time Kendra would've wanted to soak in the feeling of being in the early 1900s. Joe led them through the dining room and hovered at the back doorknob.

They each took a window on either side. "It's clear

over here," she whispered, in case the men had already entered the house. "Are you sure Beverly has another way out of this place?"

"I know her well enough to know she always has a backup plan." Joe put a finger to his lips before he opened the door. She followed him into the sticky air. The so-called bushes he'd referred to were, in reality, five-foot-tall weeds. They ran through the rest of the wild grasses and around the second house.

"Keep watch." Kendra slipped out her government-issued steel picks and made short work of the flimsy back-door lock. Joe poked his head around the corner of the house, watching for anyone coming their way. The door squeaked when she pulled on the doorknob, but they slipped inside the weathered blue house into another old kitchen, left abandoned in the middle of a remodel.

Joe joined her and closed the door behind him. "The men haven't entered her house yet. They're circling." He kept his voice soft.

Kendra peeled back the side edge of the window shade half an inch. "They've got two men approaching the back entrance." She straightened. "The house is surrounded, but I never saw Beverly exit unless she did while I picked the lock. We know there were men already at the front and side. How is she getting out?"

"She might have decided to bluff her way out. Unless Masked is sure she's betrayed them, they won't hurt her."

"How can you be so sure?"

"Your mother—"

"Please don't call her that." She closed her eyes and

exhaled. Her bones felt heavy with destroyed hopes. "I'm not ready. Beverly is so antagonistic, so bitter, so… She knows nothing about me, but she basically implied I'm bad at my job."

"Understood. It won't happen again." He nodded. "She's a hard woman, but she'd be the first to admit it. I suppose if you lived your entire adult life undercover, it might do that to a person."

Kendra prickled at the thought. She'd been undercover for several years. Already, she'd developed a thick skin and a tendency to assume the worst of people. Was Beverly a walking example of her future? "Why is she so valuable to Masked?"

"She's *the* expert at behavior analysis. The CIA recruited her because she could pinpoint with disturbing accuracy the people that were foreign agents hiding among us. When they sent her overseas, she knew who was an American agent without any prior knowledge. Back in those days, the KGB also seemed to be good at pinpointing Americans. Beverly taught our side what indicators were giving our agents away. Agents often drove the same types of cars, always took the same type of jobs—sometimes the exact same job and apartment as their predecessors."

"Does it surprise you that I can believe it? You've been in the Bureau long enough to see its flaws, maybe more so since you're an analyst. Our government excels at many things, but bureaucracy makes room for plenty of blind spots in the intelligence community."

"True, but we can thank her for a lot of the improvements that have been made since before we were born. She also pointed out where their training made them stand out in a world of other agents. Her real passion was research, though, so she retired from the CIA at a young age and continued her work in academia. That's when she met…" Joe's brow furrowed.

Kendra wasn't sure she was ready to hear any more news about her father. "If she was that good, why didn't she pick up that my father was a double agent?"

Joe removed his own sunglasses but avoided her gaze. "When I was at the Bureau, I saw enough cases where love blinded people."

Her cheeks heated so fast it took her off guard. "Well, I wouldn't know about that."

"I imagine her shame at being duped is what sent her back into Intelligence, but this time with the NCS."

"You're saying it's her way of making amends."

"If I've learned one thing today, it's not to underestimate her. I don't presume to know any of her motivations."

"So you're sure she's NCS. How do we know *she's* not the mole?"

"I think her earlier logic about taking down the communications network answered that. Besides, didn't you say all her anonymous tips helped your cases?"

She'd forgotten momentarily about that. "I'm finding it hard to believe the unfeeling woman I just met could do anything helpful without her own agenda."

"Either way, her actions don't really sound like the modus operandi of the Pirate." He peeked out the blinds. "Two more cars arrived. That's not a good sign."

"They wouldn't send so many if they were just checking on her." Kendra took another glance out the window to see for herself. "I count three from my vantage point alone. I'm sure there's more. They haven't entered the house yet." She reared back. "We can't let her be ambushed like this." She pulled her gun from the back and rushed toward the stairs. "Come on, sharpshooter."

"I shot that man only out of defense. I don't purposely kill anyone. Not anymore."

She faltered on the first step. She had a feeling he was referring to his military experience before he joined the FBI. "I appreciate that you saved my life back there. If I haven't said it before, thank you. But, Joe, I can't stand around and let Beverly get killed. I can take out most of those gunmen, but not all. I need your help."

Joe paled and reached for his weapon. "I can see that."

Kendra followed his gaze to a side window with a plate-sized rip in the shade. She'd been spotted.

Joe held his gun aim steady, certain the man outside the window couldn't see him because of the angle. "Maybe he didn't see your gun," Joe said. "Keep moving at a natural pace up the stairs."

The creak of the wood confirmed she was on the move without him looking away from the window.

"I don't think they're going to ignore potential witnesses," she said. "I can take them out from the top floor. Holler if we have a first-floor breach."

Joe blew out a steady breath, struggling to keep cool. The tension in the back of his shoulders had turned into a full-fledged knot, most likely because he refused to process what he'd done. Now, when he thought he'd never need to be responsible for someone else's physical safety again, he'd been forced to raise his weapon for the second time in one day. The man outside reached inside his blazer. Joe tensed and moved his finger closer to the trigger.

A handheld radio appeared in the man's hands as his gaze traveled above, upstairs. He was likely calling for reinforcements. He turned and waved at someone outside of Joe's view. Not good.

The windows Joe stared out of appeared to be single pane, not the double-pane windows so common after the fifties, so Joe didn't feel comfortable hollering to Kendra upstairs without fear of being heard. He took advantage of the man's distraction, though, and kept sight of him through the ten-inch-diameter hole in the shade, praying silently that the man and the "friend" who joined him didn't see Joe as he slid over to the stairway. He took the stairs three steps at a time.

He reached the landing. Kendra glanced up from her position by the northernmost window. "They haven't entered Beverly's house yet, but I'm counting a good eight men that have it surrounded now. Oh. Scratch that. One man is opening her back door." Kendra looked over her shoulder. "Why don't you take a post near the guardrail in case we get any visitors downstairs?"

"I don't intend to shoot anyone, Kendra."

She pursed her lips and glanced at the gun in his hand. "Why do you have that then?"

"For self-defense only. If you're so worried about her safety, let's call the police. Beverly made it clear she wanted us to go, and if we'd stuck to the plan—"

"You mean the plan to hide out until the coast was

clear? It wasn't as if I meant for that man to see me, Joe."

"If you weren't so intent on proving—"

Kendra's lips flattened. She lowered her weapon and stepped away from the window. With her left hand she raised an index finger. "Don't. Whatever ninja behavior analysis she taught you, I don't want to hear it. I know I'm a good agent, despite what she said. I don't need to prove anything. Besides, you didn't answer *my* question. Why do you still carry a gun?"

"I don't usually carry it."

"You had one with you at a university, Joe. I'm grateful, but that's not a normal thing for a chaplain or pastor to do."

"That's different. You saw the man who was following her. Those men are always armed."

"You appointed yourself as Beverly's personal bodyguard? Again, not the behavior of a guy ready to leave the FBI."

He opened his mouth but had no reply because he couldn't ignore the possibility she was right. Beverly had practically said the same thing when she'd suggested he keep his foot in the door by applying for the FBI chaplain program. It was like an epic game of Twister. He had one foot in law enforcement, the other foot in academia and his hands in two different types of ministry. Not a single spot felt very comfortable at the moment.

Kendra straightened and glanced out the window. "We'll have to continue this conversation later. Guard the front door. It looks like they're about to swarm both this house and Beverly's."

He rushed toward her to see if he came to the same conclusion. He was used to participating in the planning of missions, not carrying them out. Kendra saw him coming and took one step to the side. He flattened his back against the wall, beside her, as the windows upstairs had no shades. The way the sunbeams angled against the house provided some cover, though. They would reflect off the pane and make it harder for the men downstairs to know they were being watched.

"They have weapons, Joe. We can't just sit here and do nothing."

"When the FBI raids a place to take a suspect in for questioning they have weapons, too. You're not a vigilante, Kendra. Let's not go rogue. It's not time for knee-jerk reactions when we don't know their intentions."

Kendra's head fell. "Why do you have to be so logical?" Her shoulders touched his with the movement before she tilted her head to meet his gaze. Her eyes had lost the hard sheen, and he recognized a new openness to negotiation, to reason. "I feel like I'm flying blind, and I don't know what to do."

He reached over with his free hand and squeezed hers quickly before letting go. "I think we should seriously consider calling the police."

"Even if I agreed, the phone system is probably full after the shooting at the university. Doubt we can expect a fast reaction time, and she made a point of telling us not to trust anyone from other agencies. I assume that includes the police. Meanwhile, Beverly is still in there like a sitting duck."

He leaned over to look out the window. Beverly's

house burst into a flaming ball. The windows next to him exploded, blowing shards of glass inward. He grabbed Kendra and dove to the ground as the side of the house disappeared.

FOUR

Kendra hit the floor. Her knuckles made first contact. She cried out from the impact as her fingers were still wrapped around the gun. She rolled and popped up to a sitting position. Smoke billowed into the open side of the house from the massive crater next door. Half of Beverly's house was gone.

The gunmen were lying prone on the grass below. Two of them wore jackets with *FBI* on the back. Were they legit or agents on the take? Another wore a nondescript blazer and yet another had on a blue jacket with *US Marshals* in yellow letters on the back. Everything added up to confirm what Beverly and Joe had been telling her. Kendra really wouldn't be able to trust anyone until she took down the rest of Masked. One of the men started to move to his knees but fell down again. Injured but not dead, he'd likely survive.

Joe held one hand over his left ear. The jagged remains of the floor that was left beneath them creaked. He gestured to the stairs. "We need to go before this collapses, too."

Her eyes, nose and throat burned as she let her gaze

travel over the burning pile of rubble. There was too much smoke to tell just how deep the explosion went. Did it take out the basement apartment, too? "But—"

"She's not dead, Kendra. We have to go. This is our chance to escape."

She searched his soot-covered face for reassurance that he wasn't bluffing. "How do you know she's not? What if she's still in the basement, trapped? You don't know for sure, do you?"

He holstered his weapon and stood, pulling her upright with him. "No one becomes an NCS agent without always having a backup plan. She's the best of the best. The bomb was probably for our benefit so we could leave without anyone following us. Come on." Joe held her hand and guided her over the mess of broken wood and glass by the stairs, also covered in debris. The third step no longer existed.

They made it downstairs. The ringing in her ears diminished enough she could recognize the oncoming sirens—so many sirens in one day. Usually the sound spiked her adrenaline and put her on alert, but today her insides felt hollow and numb. Weeks of tracking down her birth mother only to lose her. It was hard to believe Joe's theory that she'd escaped, but he knew Beverly better than she did, so she let him lead.

For now.

They reached the same back door they'd entered. Joe unclipped his holstered gun once more and led her down an alley between old houses with detached garages. He looked over his shoulder every few steps. The gravel crunched underneath her feet. She lost track of how many turns they made before Joe came to a stop.

He checked over his shoulder once more before he accessed a garage keypad. "How are you holding up? Have you noticed any injuries?"

She focused on her breathing, and the fog that she'd operated in for the past fifteen minutes began to fade. Her bones and muscles ached from the sheer force of the explosion, but other than that, she felt fine. "No. What about you?"

He glanced down at his thumb as the garage door started to go up. "I think I got a nasty splinter but other than that—"

She snorted. She couldn't help it. "Do yourself a favor and don't lead with that injury at the next academy reunion."

He flashed the good-natured smirk that made him seem five years younger, and she found it contagious. She needed to choose to trust that Joe knew what he was talking about and keep moving forward.

The garage opened to reveal an old-fashioned cruiser bicycle with white-rimmed wheels and a basket. "You've got to be kidding me. I'll tell you right now I'm not sitting on the handles while you steer."

He waved her toward the interior door. "This is my place, a rental. The bike came with the house. I thought we could wash up, and I'll ride this to pick up my car and come back to pick get you. If you don't mind, I'd like to grab a bag before we travel to Caltech."

The statement brought back the sense of urgency. "You have a go bag ready, right?"

He nodded. "Some habits die hard."

She suspected it was more that he wasn't really ready to leave the FBI, but she didn't want to start that discussion again. "Between the shooting on campus and the house exploding, I would imagine all the ways out of town will be guarded checkpoints in no time flat. While I think we could pass inspection, I'd rather not increase Masked's chances in discovering I was the Fed who contacted Beverly."

"I'm not worried about the checkpoints. I know of a farm with an access road that leads clear out to a highway. I'll be shocked if anyone thinks to monitor that."

She reached up and brushed the soot off his cheek without thinking. He stiffened but looked down, a kindness in his eyes that made her heart beat faster. She pulled her hand back as if burned. "Sorry. I'm sure you can take care of that yourself." What was wrong with her?

"I'll take all the help I can get." He shrugged. "I don't pay much attention to my appearance."

As if. His clothes always looked brand-new, crisp and fresh. She gestured toward his button-down shirt that amazingly, despite the soot covering it, didn't look wrinkled.

"I find ironing to be relaxing, and I like starch." He opened the door inside his house. "Restroom is to your left. I'll grab my car first and we can either leave town or get your rental, though I think the campus will be on lockdown."

"I parked on a side street."

"Smart. Should've known you would've." He strode in the house and up the stairs while she stepped in the spotless washroom. Her apartment was barely lived in and wasn't this clean. She didn't think the adage "cleanliness is next to godliness" was actually in the Bible, but it probably didn't hurt as a quality trait on his résumé if he really was making a transition to being a pastor. Kendra made sure all evidence of ash and grime was removed from herself and the sink. Once she got her bag from her car she would have to change clothes at the airport to ensure no one smelled smoke on her before boarding.

She stepped out and Joe stood waiting, holding a bag in one hand and offering her a water bottle in the other. It was as if they'd both switched on autopilot. Within fifteen minutes, they'd returned his car to the garage and managed to escape town in her rental, even though they'd passed plenty of parked police cruisers and black SUVs, likely assigned to federal agents. They both kept their hats and sunglasses on despite the overcast skies, until Joe found the dirt access road on barren farmland that had already been harvested.

Another sixty minutes later, they returned the rental at the airport and bought separate tickets on Southwest with direct service to Los Angeles. Since there was no assigned seating on the airline, they could sit together without fear of someone looking at the manifest and connecting the dots. By the time the attendant announced boarding, they'd gone three hours without speaking, which was fine with her.

"You know what I remember most at the academy?" Joe asked, as if he'd heard her thoughts and wanted to correct her. He leaned back in his seat, ignoring the flight attendant's safety speech. "Boxing."

She cringed. "I have a lot of memories of Quantico, but that's one of many I definitely choose to forget most of the time." The boxing test was a necessary, but painful, part of training. All trainees had been paired up in a boxing ring, men against women, and told to beat on each other in order to prove they could defend themselves. "I'll never forget that poor accountant. Cynthia, was it?"

He groaned. "Brandon popped her right in the nose, and that was it. She quit." He shook his head and sneaked a glance at her. "I wouldn't have lasted, either, if I hadn't been paired with you."

"Maybe."

"No, I'm sure. I'll never forget tapping you on the shoulder while the instructor yelled to hit you harder. If you hadn't made it clear you knew how to defend yourself with that fake-out jump punch to my jaw, I wouldn't have passed." He shook his head. "I still don't agree with that part of our training. If I'd actually made any contact with you or caused any bruises like some of the others…"

"You can thank my three older brothers and my Tang Soo Do instructors. I had to be an expert in wrestling and blocking maneuvers."

"I'm pretty sure that's what you told me back then, too."

She found herself smiling, not at the memory of having to fight each other, but from remembering what happened afterward. "I never thought I would be consoling a guy who tried to hit me—even though I totally know you took it easy on me—with burgers and fries."

He laughed. "I felt horrible. Never thought I would ever try to hit a girl, even if it was for training." His smile morphed into a frown. "I think that was when I first questioned whether I'd taken the right path."

There he went again, implying he was serious about leaving the FBI. She refused to believe it. "I'm sorry I got you wrapped up in this. Obviously, it's not normal FBI work, so you can't really judge—"

"You heard Beverly. She had this in mind for me ever since I met her, just shortly after I arrived as the interim associate pastor. I was just too trusting to see it."

Kendra chose her words carefully because she knew—despite the loud aircraft noise—that someone might overhear bits and pieces of their conversation. "But if you hadn't needed to help me this morning, she might not have been able to manipulate you into coming with me. For that, I'm sorry."

He leaned slightly toward her so only she could hear. "There's no need to apologize. While I stood in line, I realized that it wouldn't have mattered." His voice was soft and caring. "All Beverly would've needed to do was mention your name, and I'd have come running. I think she knew that."

Kendra felt her eyes widen but didn't reply. What did he mean? Because they could never, ever, be more than friends no matter how strong the attraction. Agents together as a couple never worked.

He clenched his jaw and looked down as if he'd said too much before he leaned back and closed his eyes.

Joe thought he managed to act nonchalant the rest of the way to Los Angeles and even through the insanity of renting a car and driving to Pasadena from LAX in rush-hour traffic. Inwardly, though, he worried that his admission to Kendra sent the wrong message. Her eyes widened as if he'd just proclaimed romantic intentions, but if he tried to correct her and explain that he just meant he would do anything for his friends, that would just add fuel to the fire. He would have sounded desperate, like a man who had said "I love you" without hearing it back. No, the right thing to do was to let it go and act cool.

Even though the drive was only supposed to be a little over twenty miles, the trip took over two hours. He blew out a forceful breath as he finally got to California Boulevard. "So, you never told me, what was it like to meet your sister for the first time? I mean besides being shocked."

She tilted her head from side to side as if considering how much to share. "Well, I had a scheduled meet with a contact, but bullets started flying before I could get there. I was trying not to let on that I'd been shot so I might not have been thinking clearly. Mostly, I needed to understand why my partner was running with someone who looked identical to me before I acknowledged I needed help. I had no idea what was going on."

The news almost made him pull over. "What?"

"I didn't want to get into it with Beverly, especially since we were short on time, but I didn't meet Audrey inside a conference like she intended. It was a mission gone wrong. I was in the middle of trying to get the answers I wanted when I passed out, hit my head and ended up in surgery. When I woke up, Audrey had taken my place on the mission. She was actually the one with my partner, Lee, who took down the communications of Masked."

"Whoa. I'm glad they got you into surgery in time."

Kendra smiled. "So you really didn't know about

that? It may sound weird, but it brings me a little solace that Beverly doesn't know everything."

He couldn't imagine what she had to feel like knowing Beverly had kept tabs on her for all her life, but had never reached out.

"Anyway, to answer your question, I didn't really process that I had a twin until I woke up in the hospital with nothing to do but wait for updates from Lee and Audrey. After the fact, though, I—I guess it's almost like finding a part of myself I'd been missing." She shook her head. "That probably sounds melodramatic. I love my adoptive family. I can't imagine if someone else had raised me." She held up a hand as if shaking the thought away. "We're here." Her voice changed to a businesslike tone.

"I have brothers. I can't imagine what it would feel like to meet them as adults."

She shrugged. "Audrey and I are very different people, but we've discovered a few areas of similar taste. Well, you're about to see for yourself." She glanced at him. "I know it's dark already, but I think we should keep the hats on in case someone is watching for us. Audrey lives in faculty housing just ahead."

"Understood." He parked and stepped out of the vehicle. Behind them, many of the undergrad houses were decked out in Christmas lights, but as they crossed the campus they passed a hundred-foot-tall building, where strings of sixty-foot rope lights formed the shape of a Christmas tree that reached the rooftop. "Does your sister know we're coming?"

"I texted her at the airport that I needed to speak to her in person, urgently. She should be waiting for me."

They rounded a corner to find floating bright lights racing toward them. "What—"

Joe operated on instinct and grabbed Kendra by the shoulders, tugging her off the path into the grass, before a group of almost a hundred bikes almost ran them over.

"Sorry, Professor Clark," someone called out.

"Come with us, Professor," another student shouted, glancing back toward them briefly. "Christmas light ride!"

"You have to see Christmas Tree Lane," another bicyclist shouted.

Kendra awkwardly held up a hand in a wave but didn't answer. Two minutes later the path was empty. She grimaced. "So much for keeping a low profile. If they know Audrey is engaged, we might've started some rumors."

His mind drifted to what it would be like to pretend to be a couple with Kendra, but he refocused as she'd started walking again. The thought did trigger a question, though. "Are you okay with your twin getting married to your partner?"

"Former partner," she corrected. "Lee is getting transferred to be an FBI recruiter at UCLA soon, to be closer to her." She smiled, and maybe he wanted to believe it, but the gesture seemed genuine. "Lee's like one of my brothers. Like I said, Audrey and I are *very* different people. I don't know how she could see him as anything more, but I'm genuinely happy for them. If there was any jealousy it's only that I'm pretty sure they're going to live happily-ever-after." She sighed. "And how often does that happen?"

He wanted to ask if she ever hoped for a happily-ever-after and what type of man she'd look for, as a natural continuation of the conversation. But, given the awkwardness after the plane ride, he decided to keep his follow-up questions to himself. "I've met Lee before. It's been a few years, but he seems like a great guy."

She reached the bottom steps of the apartment building. "Is that your professional opinion as an analyst?"

"I didn't profile him, but I'm typically 70 percent right about a person based on my first impression, yeah."

"Isn't that 30 percent room for error the most important part?"

"If your sister is anything like you, I'm sure she's made a smart choice."

That prompted another smile. "She *is* smart. Obviously. Or we wouldn't be here." They took the stairs to the second floor. Kendra hesitated at the top and spun around to face him. "Listen, the focus is on stopping the Pirate. We aren't going to bring up Beverly again until Audrey is gone."

"Are you sure? That's a pretty big piece of the puzzle to leave out." It was true he didn't know for sure that Beverly had survived the blast, but he preferred to remain optimistic.

Her eyes narrowed, ever so slightly. "It's not my place or even my right to explain our birth mother works for the NCS. Audrey loves to gather facts and develop hypotheses. She'd have made an excellent interrogator, and I can't take the time to rehash every word and gesture Beverly made today. Besides, Beverly seemed to think Audrey wasn't in danger at the moment. I think the safest route for Audrey is to keep information on a need-to-know basis."

While Beverly had told him about her daughters under the guise of having a crisis of faith, she hadn't talked about their careers. He found it interesting that each daughter seemed to excel at elements of Beverly's job. One was a researcher while the other was a covert agent. "Information on a need-to-know basis," he answered. "Got it."

Her shoulders dropped with an exhale. She nodded, then took two more steps until she reached an apartment door covered up by a wreath dotted with Disney characters wearing lab coats and safety glasses. Her forehead wrinkled in confusion. "What—"

Joe couldn't help but smile at the cute display, as Kendra had probably stopped at the wrong door. She wasn't the type of person to take part in holiday decorations, and as near as he remembered, she wasn't a big fan of Christmas.

The door in question swung open and Joe felt his eyebrows jump. There were two Kendras in front of him, except only one of them wore an ugly Christmas sweater and a jubilant smile while bouncing on her toes.

"I thought that was you outside." The twin wrapped her arms around Kendra's neck while simultaneously pulling her inside the apartment. "I was so happy to get your text. Did you find her?"

"I honestly don't know where our birth mother is, but that's not why I'm here." Kendra shook her head slightly and stepped out of the embrace, but her eyes were wide and dazed as she looked around the apartment.

Joe stepped inside the threshold, without asking, curious what he'd see. The smell of cinnamon and nutmeg hit him first as an oven timer beeped. Every wall in the apartment was covered with Christmas decorations. In the corner, a tree was so full of lights he almost needed sunglasses to look at it. Even the windows were outlined in lights, but the blinds were pulled open to see the outdoors. That was how Audrey had known they were coming. He crossed the room and closed the blinds. Someone else could be watching. If news got to the Pirate that Audrey had a twin, their chance to lure him into the open would disappear.

"Uh, who is this?" Audrey asked in a cheerful voice, her green eyes full of consternation that a strange man was taking such a liberty in her apartment.

Joe tipped his cap and opened his mouth to introduce himself but Kendra gestured toward him first.

"This is Joe Rose. He's my partner for a last-minute mission, and I'm afraid we're here to ask for your help."

Audrey bounced over to the oven, seemingly nonplussed, as she pulled out a baking sheet of gingerbread men and turned off the timer. "You need me to pretend to be you again?" She smiled. "Because I've gotten pretty good at it, if I do say so myself."

"Actually, no. I need to take *your* place."

Her smile faded, and she didn't turn from staring at the oven. "That's a big ask. You know my research is classified."

"So was my mission to stop the Masked Network."

Audrey grabbed a spatula and started transferring the cookies to a cooling rack. She gave a side-glance to Joe. "Are you any good with icing?"

That took him off guard. "Um, maybe?"

"Good. Because I think my sister is going to have a lot harder time pretending to be me than the other way around."

Kendra barked a laugh. "I'm trained to do under-cover work, Audrey."

"Hmm. We'll see. If you wouldn't mind taking over…" Audrey picked up an icing packet and handed it to Joe. "Outline these men, dots for eyes, a smiley face and three cinnamon buttons down the torso." She finally turned to Kendra. "It sounds like we have a lot to talk about while your new partner works on these."

"We can talk in front of him. He's trustworthy."

"But this is my research, and I can't take your word for it." She held up a hand. "No offense, Joe." She approached her sister. "Besides, if I go along with this switcheroo, which I assume you have good reason for, I need to know you can pull it off." Audrey stuck out a thumb in Joe's direction. "And he can be the one to prove it."

Joe sensed a test in the making, and he wasn't sure how to study.

FIVE

Kendra knew it wouldn't be easy, she just didn't realize Audrey would be so stubborn, even after she'd explained the situation. "I'm not sure you understand—"

"I understand the stakes." Audrey paced in front of
the queen bed draped in a dark blue coverlet covered
in snowflakes. "I just need a moment to digest it, especially since you're asking me not to tell Lee about any
of this." She rolled her eyes and blew out a breath. "It
seems wrong to keep secrets from my fiancé."

"I know it's awkward, but the less either of you know,
the better. It keeps both you and us safer. My source…"
Speaking of keeping things from loved ones, Kendra
fought back a guilty conscience. She'd broach the topic
of their mother after the research was safe and the Pirate
was behind bars. Although now, after seeing Audrey in
her element, she wondered if Audrey received the academic and positive qualities both their biological parents must've had while Kendra was given the cold, dark
sides, destined to live a life of deceit and loneliness.

"Your source?" Audrey prompted.

She blinked away the stray thought. "My source told

me that the influence of the Pirate is pervasive. We don't know who to trust."

Her mouth dropped open. "You're not saying you suspect Lee—"

"No, of course not. I trusted Lee with my life…and with my sister." Kendra smiled and Audrey seemed appeased. "My request stands, though. Please don't even tell him you're leaving the campus. Maybe go to your parents for a visit but keep it low-key. Make sure they don't announce it to anyone."

"Well, I was pretty stressed last time I spoke to them." She blew out a breath. "It wouldn't be a stretch to tell them I was nearing burnout and just need some quiet R and R a few days earlier than planned. I was going to see them at the end of semester."

Even the nightstand held a small Christmas tree. "I have to ask you, what's with Christmas exploding in your place?"

Audrey's intense look of concentration disappeared. "What do you mean? Don't you decorate for the holidays?" Her expression morphed into one of pity. "Oh, I forgot. Deep cover. You probably didn't have time or any decorations of your own."

Even if she had, Kendra would've never bothered, but she was curious why her sister was so passionate. There was so much they still didn't know about each other. "What were the holidays like for you growing up?" Kendra asked.

"The day after Thanksgiving, my parents would pull out a jar with roughly twenty-five days worth of Christmas activities, usually filled with a lot of homemade decoration instructions, movie names to watch and recipes to make. I loved it. Why? What was it like for you?"

"Well, I wasn't an only child like you. I mean, it was fine, but since my three brothers were all biological and I was adopted, I always felt... I don't know. The holidays seemed to magnify that I was different. Not their fault—they didn't say or do anything wrong—but when extended family came over, that's how I felt." The memories weren't all bad, though. In fact, one memory still made Kendra laugh. "My mom did try to get me to help her make cookies and decorations, but I didn't think it was fair. I just wanted to be outside throwing a football with my brothers."

Audrey's eyes filled with an understanding she couldn't possibly know.

The sensation unnerved her. "Anyway, I wish I could give you time to weigh the pros and cons of hiding at your parents', but we need to find the Pirate's identity before he finds out mine. I need you out of here so I can take your place, pronto. I'm up against the clock."

Audrey spun to the dresser and pulled out a green, tissue-wrapped bundle. "I have a present for you. And, since it sounds like there's no other option, I think you need it sooner than later." She shoved the package into Kendra's arms.

She tried to follow Audrey's train of thought but failed. "I didn't get you a present. It's not Christmas yet."

"It's for the mission."

Kendra felt her face scrunch in confusion. "But you didn't know about the mission until now."

Audrey rolled her eyes. "Just open it."

Kendra sighed and ripped apart the tissue paper to

discover a replica of the ridiculous sweater Audrey was wearing. It portrayed a reindeer on the front wearing a sweater—a sweater within a sweater—with tinsel wrapped around its antlers. "You've got to be kidding."

"I'm assuming this is your first ugly Christmas sweater. You're going to love it. More important, you need to embrace the Christmas spirit or no one is going to believe you're me. Now let's get your hair pulled back—I'll hurry and straighten mine so we match—and see if that handsome man you clearly have a crush on can tell the difference between the two of us."

Her cheeks burned. "First of all, we are friends and colleagues and nothing more. And I didn't bring him here to help you decorate."

"He seemed happy to help."

For some reason it annoyed Kendra that Audrey had pegged him correctly. "He's probably the most helpful man alive, but—"

"And it's a very relaxing activity." Audrey crossed her arms.

"Maybe for you."

"Sounds to me like someone needs a lesson in holiday fun."

Kendra forced down a growl that threatened to surface. While they often seemed to get into small rounds of bickering ever since they'd met, as if making up for lost time in the sibling-rivalry department, they needed to focus. "Second, this isn't a game."

Audrey stilled and a fierceness Kendra recognized replaced the smile from a moment ago. "Believe me, I understand. If the Pirate is really the mastermind of Masked, I have an inkling of what he's capable of, but

I'm not sure *you* understand that if it gets out I let my sister take my place in the lab, my reputation, my grant and my career will be ruined." She ticked off three fingers in a row for emphasis. "Besides that, I'm responsible for all those grad students, postdocs and technicians who work for me." Her index finger jabbed in the air, pointing over Kendra's shoulder as if the people she listed were standing behind them. "If you discover the Pirate's identity without capturing him, he's going to kill anyone in my lab that can point the finger at him."

"I'm well aware of the dangers." Kendra studied the floor and tried to shut down her defensive streak. "I will admit I wasn't thinking about the risks to your future, but, Audrey, you took my place. I think I can handle taking yours. I'm actually trained to do this sort of thing."

Audrey sank on the edge of her bed. "When I was you, I had Lee by my side. He'd been your partner for ages and knew you enough to offer me help when I needed to be convincing. You have Joe. He seems nice, but he doesn't know me. And, I'd venture to say that while we've been getting to know each other, you don't know me as well as the lab staff that's with me seven days a week, without fail."

Kendra wasn't ready to admit that her sister had given this a lot of thought. So instead, she sighed. "Fine. I'll agree to your test. I can't believe you got me a matching sweater."

Audrey's face relaxed. "It was first on my twin bucket list."

Kendra gaped. "You have a bucket list for us?"

"Don't you?" Audrey stepped forward and grabbed both of Kendra's hands, pulling them together. "I don't mean to complicate things, but I have some news. Big news." Her eyes looked directly into Kendra's. "You know how you asked that we wait until you returned to get married?"

She felt her eyes grow wide. Had they already gotten hitched?

"Lee and I took a guess that you would be back by Christmas either way so we've planned a small wedding. Family only. It's time we meet each other's parents, don't you think? I know my parents can't wait to meet you. They'll have you loving the holidays within ten minutes of meeting them."

Kendra's mouth dropped open. "Uh…wow. Congratulations."

Audrey pulled her into a tight hug. Kendra closed her eyes tight. The hits just kept on coming. She wasn't ready to admit to Audrey that she hadn't even told her parents yet that she'd discovered a twin sister. She wanted to have more information, more answers, before she presented such big news to her law-enforcement family.

Audrey pulled back and her eyes glistened with excitement. "If you could make sure no one is trying to kill you by Christmas Eve, that would be great."

Kendra's mouth went dry. "So no pressure."

Joe stepped back from his work. Some of the gingerbread men had buttons that resembled tears, but at least he got most of the smiles right. At the sound of footsteps approaching, he turned to find two identical sisters in front of him. They stared at him wordlessly, and he knew they were waiting for him to take a guess.

No contest.

While they both wore the best Christmas sweater he'd ever seen and matching jeans, Kendra had her eyebrows raised, which made her eyes look a little bigger. They held a distinct lack of amusement. She tucked her chin while averting her gaze and pulled back her shoulders. A textbook set of cues for flirting but Joe wouldn't let himself believe that's what she was doing. Kendra was anything but textbook.

More likely, she was sending confusing signals on purpose in the hope he'd guess wrong. But, he had to admit bias. He felt a spark, one he couldn't explain, when he looked at Kendra. And clearly it wasn't dependent on how she looked because Audrey looked—obviously—just as pretty.

"To be fair, you know I study people, right?" He gestured and looked left at Audrey before he waved toward the cookies. "I tried my best, Audrey, but I'm not a skilled decorator. You might not want to trust me with the rest."

Kendra sagged. "How'd you know who was who?"

If he voiced aloud his thoughts, the amount of awkwardness in the room would increase tenfold. "Let's just say I know you better than you think." He suddenly noticed Audrey's hand and pointed. "It would also help if the engaged woman in the room wasn't wearing a diamond."

Kendra's smile was triumphant as she spun toward her sister. "Okay. So you cheated. I'm going to need that ring."

"Not a chance." Audrey held her hand to her chest. "I take off my ring before I go to work. I have a strict policy against jewelry because of some of the equipment. No one at the lab ever sees the ring so it stays with me." She eyed both of them. "Before I agree to this swap, I have questions. Why now? Why would the Pirate go after my research now?"

Joe waited a beat for Kendra to answer but she looked conflicted, perhaps about what to reveal, so he jumped in. "There are rumors going around in the intelligence community that you are near a breakthrough of sorts."

Audrey rolled her eyes. "In my field, we call gossip 'collaboration.' But for classified research, I would expect scientists and engineers to be a little more tight-lipped. It's easy enough for it to happen, though. While the research data itself is classified, we're encouraged to be fostering a spirit of teamwork. This university is a tight-knit community so it's probably to be expected."

"Is there anyone in your lab we should suspect? Someone who might be getting paid to leak these kinds of details?" Kendra asked.

"No. I mean if there were, it wouldn't be the first time a postdoc researcher transmitted information to another party, but I don't think anyone in my lab fits that mold."

"Your research grant is defense-related," Joe said. "The rumor said something about invisibility cloaks?"

Kendra snickered. "It was invisibility and cloaking," she corrected.

Audrey didn't crack a smile. "Please. Tons of labs have made invisibility cloaks."

Joe gaped. If he could get his hands on one, he could just imagine the well-earned pranks he could play on his brother.

"But it's not like you might imagine, so put the subject out of your mind. I'm using metamaterials, nano-technology and optics to make something a little more commercially viable. Let's just say we hope to produce something that can cloak sound as well as visibility. So I'll agree to allow you in my lab, but the data needs to stay secure."

Audrey crossed the apartment to retrieve her purse. "I have what I need on a flash drive at all times, but you need to secure my office hard drive. My staff focuses on their assigned tasks, but I'm the only one who sees how everything ties together." She eyed Joe. "Lee was supposed to come for a visit in a couple weeks, right before Christmas. I already jumped through the hoops to get him a security badge so he could meet everyone. We'll just say he came early if you're okay with acting the part of a doting fiancé."

Joe tempered his response to not sound overeager. "I think we can manage. Kendra is experienced at acting like part of a married couple. I'll follow her lead."

Audrey regarded him. "Yes, but engaged couples are a little more doting on each other. They *look* in love. At least we do. And Lee and I both love the holidays. I've talked about it enough with my coworkers that they'll know."

Kendra pursed her lips and narrowed her eyes at Audrey. "Let us worry about the cover situation. Are you saying the rumor about you getting close to a break-through isn't true?"

"I didn't say that." Audrey's lips curved to one side. She clearly had a juicy secret. "If the rumor is going around, though, it explains why I had a last-minute request for a tour."

Joe frowned. "A tour?"

"Right after Kendra let me know she was on the way here, the request came through. It's not that unusual for the government to want to check in on progress and review how the funds are being used, understandable when they're providing me with an eight-million-dollar grant."

Joe felt his eyes bulge but realized that probably wasn't a huge amount given the type of research.

"What is a little odd is the short notice from DARPA on who is visiting the lab tomorrow," Audrey added.

The Defense Advanced Research Projects Agency was sending people? That could be the Pirate's connection to the research. "So you got the list of who is visiting?"

"A couple of people from the Department of Defense as well as a couple scientists from a few related research labs DARPA has in the works. I've already secured them passes." She picked up a stack of smart cards attached to lanyards from the desk in the corner and handed them to Joe. "I'm supposed to meet them outside the lab at ten in the morning."

Joe's and Kendra's eyes met. The timing of the tour request couldn't be ignored. "Good thing we came straight here." He picked up one of the three burner phones he'd purchased with a Visa gift card, thanks to Beverly's stash, at the airport kiosk and handed it to Audrey. "Keep this on at all times in case we need to ask you a question—I imagine there will be some as we secure your research."

Kendra pointed at the phone's screen. "If you receive a text from Joe or me, we will end the message with the number *2* and an asterisk so you know it's from us. Whenever you text me reply with a—"

"With a *100%* because I'm behind you one—"

"We don't need to choose meanings behind our codes, but sure." Kendra took a deep breath and looked at Joe. She paled slightly. "I think we're about to meet the Pirate."

SIX

Kendra had never needed so much coffee. They'd stayed awake until three in the morning as Audrey mercilessly drilled them on "just enough" lab procedures and vague go-to answers until she was satisfied the swap wouldn't ruin her research and career. Kendra then handed her fake identification to show at the airport while Joe supplied the car rental keys and Visa gift cards to pay for Audrey's flight.

Now, a little after nine, the burner phone buzzed with confirmation Audrey had made it to her childhood home in Michigan. Kendra checked the clock. The DARPA review team would arrive at the lab in thirty minutes. She needed to beat everyone there to get her bearings.

Joe stepped out of the bathroom, shaved and dressed in an emerald green button-down shirt. He looked annoyingly chipper given he'd had a sleepless night, as well. He glanced at Kendra and clearly fought back a laugh. "Suits you. Festive."

She knew he was referring to her one-button red blazer covered in images of snowmen, reindeer and evergreen trees. "If Audrey hadn't bragged to her techs that she was wearing this for the review, I could dress like a normal person. At least when she had to pretend to be me, it was either lounge pants or designer outfits."

"Embrace your cover."

She felt herself roll her eyes.

He laughed, a deep, rich chuckle that took her off guard. "How one thinks about the mission affects how one performs the mission." He dropped the professor voice and handed her the lanyard that had a red Christmas bell attached. "You're supposed to love Christmas. You might even start to believe it." Joe winked and lifted the tray of gingerbread cookies. "Allow me. Lead the way."

They reached the engineering lab building and walked down an empty hallway until they reached a biohazard caution sign outside a nondescript door, just as Audrey had described. A loud click sounded, followed by a short beep. Joe reached across and opened the door with his free hand. The microchip in the security badges attached to their lanyards granted them access without having to touch anything or prove themselves to security guards.

Inside, the automatic lights flickered on and Kendra felt like she was back in school, fulfilling a general-education requirement. Several freestanding counters stood in the center of the room with stools waiting for lab techs. Beyond that, the setting looked nothing like her memories of science courses.

"There should be a log of everyone that entered and exited using the RFID microchip system," Joe said. "We should take a look at it sometime today and look for anomalies." He crossed the room to two units attached to the wall that resembled industrial-sized incubation units, like you'd see for newborns, except there were giant oven fan hoods attached to the top. "To catch fumes," Joe said. He nodded toward the cabinets. "Flammable and chemical cabinet storage below it."

His analyst brain had latched onto the host of procedures, regulations, processing standards and statues demanded of a proper research lab. While she'd initially resented it, Kendra was relieved Beverly had planned for him to help. He had understood everything Audrey had explained.

Kendra strode to the door labeled Principal Investigator. The title seemed appropriate for her role undercover, but Audrey had explained it was actually the given title for a person in charge of the research.

Joe strode ahead of her and held up his lanyard to the office door. Nothing happened. "Just checking to see if she was right about her desk and hard drive being secure."

Kendra held up Audrey's lanyard and it opened right away. In the corner, a small, fake Christmas tree was set up. Even at work! Joe set down the cookies on the only clear spot on the wraparound countertop that served as one giant desk. Stacks of academic journals and file folders threatened to topple at the slightest movement, and sticky notes were plastered on every other surface, including the laptop. A black box, likely the external hard drive, was free of dust and paper, as if it was the only object in the office treated with respect. She fingered the cable that connected the external hard drive to a bolt in the wall. A similar cable secured the computer that could only be freed by the keys she held in her pocket.

Audrey had promised she could secure and move the data stored in the school's server location to a new virtual location, but Kendra would have to be responsible for securing the physical data. As soon as the tour was done, she would secure the research, wipe the computers and give all the techs the unusual gift of the lab being closed for the holidays.

"Let's get the lay of the land before people start arriving," Joe said.

She made sure the office door clicked behind them. The lab wasn't just one room but several. Each door opened to a new section, many filled with massive equipment. "They look like giant deconstructed microscopes and sets of electronic drums."

Joe laughed. "I feel pretty certain they're not drums."

"Is this Lee?" a chipper voice asked from behind them.

Kendra spun around to find a petite woman with a brown-haired pixie cut, the tips frosted, already in a lab coat with safety glasses in her hand. "Shannon," Kendra said aloud. It had to be Audrey's right-hand tech, unless there was more than one worker with spiky hair as her sister had described. When the woman smiled, Kendra figured she'd guessed right. "I'd like you to meet my fiancé."

Joe offered a hearty handshake with his right hand. "Good to meet you," he said. Kendra flinched, though, when he put his left hand around her shoulders. "Audrey here—" he squeezed her shoulder again and Kendra fought back a laugh "—talks about you all the time."

Shannon beamed. "Well, I would hope so since we eat, sleep and breathe most of our life away in here. Though, to be fair, I've heard a lot about you, too."

"All good, I hope."

"No one's perfect, Lee." She blinked hard, without any hint of humor.

Kendra snorted. She couldn't help it. Audrey had mentioned that some of her staff had quirks. Blatant honesty was supposed to be Shannon's claim to fame. She wondered what Audrey had said that indicated Lee wasn't perfect? And even though Audrey claimed Shannon couldn't possibly be susceptible to a recruiter like the Pirate, the extreme honesty could be faked easily enough. Some might even call the trait endearing and use the technique to build trust.

"That's true," Joe answered, a good-natured smile on his face. "I know I have faults."

"There's a guy waiting outside the lab." Shannon hitched a finger over her shoulder. "He says you're expecting him. Your ex-boyfriend."

Joe's eyebrows hopped an inch. "Is that so?"

Kendra fought to keep the surprise from her face. "I don't recall anything about an ex-boyfriend due to arrive today." Did Audrey have many ex-boyfriends?

Shannon's nose wrinkled. "You said he was coming in two weeks. I assumed if Lee came early, he would, too."

"On the same day as the tour review, though? Not ideal." Kendra glanced at the digital clock mounted on the far-side wall.

"Do you want me to get the security pass from your office? It was approved last week, I think."

She exchanged a glance with Joe. So Shannon had access to Audrey's office? If the tech had any hacking skills, that meant the data wasn't as safe as Audrey had insinuated. "That's okay. I have a quick phone call to make, anyway. Shannon, would you mind taking Lee around the rest of the lab and giving him the full tour? Consider it a practice round. I'd like you to give the DARPA team the tour, as well."

Her eyes widened. "You want me to give the tour? Is that really a good idea?"

After the proof-of-honesty bit, Kendra wasn't so sure, but Audrey had seemed to think it a better solution than practicing for several more hours until Kendra sounded more convincing. "Yes. I'm sure. I'll be standing by."

Shannon nodded and turned to Joe. "So before I start, how much do you know about shadow-sphere lithography and nanoscale patterns?"

Joe's lips pressed together and his eyebrows jumped, but he didn't object as Kendra made her way back to the office. Once the door was closed, she flipped open the burner phone and reached Audrey in five seconds flat.

"What happened to no phone calls unless it's an emergency? I was just starting to fall asleep. I got no sleep on the plane thanks to a cute but very loud baby."

"This constitutes an emergency. I need information. The military research review team is due to arrive in fifteen minutes. Explain to me why your ex-boyfriend is here."

"Wyatt?" Disbelief coated Audrey's voice. "Why is everyone showing up so early?"

"So it's true he was expected?"

An exaggerated sigh came across the line. "Yes.

He requested a visit about a month ago. Don't worry, though. He has clearance. They sent me his badge like, a week ago. It's in my top drawer. And before you object, Lee knew all about Wyatt coming. I even asked to make sure he would be there when Wyatt visited so there wouldn't be any need for jealousy. Though, I had no idea he would just show up early without warning."

"Is that what this is about? Is this Wyatt guy here to lure you back?"

"No, of course not. Well, I mean I don't think so. He knows I'm engaged."

"Then what do I need to know about him?" Kendra asked. "My understanding is he's waiting in the hallway."

"His full name is Wyatt Nardelli, and you can cross him off your suspect list because he can't be your guy. He's a bit older than me, but the most brilliant man you'll meet. He's already had a few successful government research grants. He also served as my sounding board when I first had the idea years ago. Oh, and you need to be extra careful pretending to be me when you're around him."

"Because he's the most brilliant man I'll meet. Got it." She wondered if Lee was the jealous type. Her former partner didn't seem to be, but she'd never seen him in love, either.

"No, because he's my ex-boyfriend. Five years ago, he knew me very well. If he calls you out on anything maybe you can tell him that people change."

Ah. Right.

"Let's see what do you need to know? His favorite movie is *The Princess Bride*, but who doesn't love that?

He listens to country music, which in my opinion was reason enough to break up." She laughed.

"What was the real reason you broke up?" Kendra asked.

"Moved away. Lab work makes it hard enough to keep a relationship going. Especially when I was still in postdoctoral research at Duke. Some compare it to indentured servitude. Add in distance, and it became impossible. I never took any time off, so I could never visit him, and video chats never felt natural. Though, I'm totally willing to do that for Lee, so I probably just didn't like him enough." She yawned and Kendra fought against its contagiousness. "Just be friendly and get Shannon to give him the tour so you don't have to worry about interacting much."

Shannon to the rescue yet again. There were too many people arriving weeks earlier than expected, trying to gain access in the lab at the same time. The sudden review from DARPA was suspicious enough, but add the ex-boyfriend and the fact that Beverly said rumors had already been flying around—it all added up to a conclusion that made Kendra antsy. "Audrey, I'm starting to wonder if you've been straight with me. You're not simply near a discovery, are you? Have you already had a significant breakthrough?"

Audrey's momentary silence hit the mark. "If this all goes south I still need to prove that I did my best to keep the research classified. I really wish you wouldn't ask me specifics."

Kendra groaned, but at least she had her answer. "Okay, fine. But tell me this. Does your staff know you already have? They've helped you all along, right?"

"They have suspicions. I told them to expect big news this week. That was the other reason for bringing cookies, but like I said, just tell them the big news is we're shutting down the lab for the holidays. If the DARPA team is there, I'll leave the data up for thirty minutes, then I'll move it from the cloud. You'll take care of the hard copy."

Kendra knew the plan because they'd gone over it until they'd been blue in the face. She said goodbye and opened the door to find the lab had filled with people, all Audrey's age or younger. She tried to smile, but as she flashed her teeth, it felt like more of a grimace.

The hired postdocs in the room were just as Audrey described. There was a male in his late twenties with curly hair, a tall redhead with a curved back stooping over a tool that resembled a microscope and a blonde with black glasses—the only one that resembled most stock photos of scientists. Others trickled in, watching her, maybe waiting for the announcement.

Kendra used her best teacher voice to speak loud enough so that everyone could hear her. "As you know, I said I had some news."

One lab tech pumped a fist, as if he already knew what she was going to say. That could be problematic. Maybe Audrey wasn't as tight-lipped as she'd indicated. "After this tour, the lab will be closing for the holidays for a security upgrade. You will still be paid."

Eyebrows raised, mouths dropped open. This definitely wasn't the news they expected. The fist pumper recovered his initial surprise and shouted, "Merry Christmas to me!"

The blonde frowned. "Are you okay with that? Won't that slow things down?"

Shannon held up a cell phone, effectively providing Kendra with an excuse not to answer. "Bradley is waiting outside the door to let everyone in. He says all the DARPA people are here. Shall I tell him to bring them in?"

"I will. Thank you." Kendra crossed the lab and opened the door to a well-dressed group in professional clothing, a stark difference to her ridiculous Christmas blazer. Her cheeks flushed at the thought as a smoldering smile and deep brown eyes, filled with awareness, flashed in her direction. "Wyatt," she said.

He beamed and leaned a little too close for comfort. "I'll just join the tour until we can get a moment alone," he said conspiratorially.

Kendra really should've insisted that Audrey hand over her engagement ring. Now would be a good time to casually touch her face and show off the diamond's sparkle as a reminder for the guy to keep his distance. Instead, she straightened and addressed the eager group, knowing full well that one of the people she was about to let in could be the Pirate.

From a corner of the room, Joe watched the group file into the lab. He intended to stay out of the way to properly analyze. It was hard to focus, though, as a man placed his hand on Kendra's lower back and stepped to her side. Joe didn't need any baseline behaviors to gather the man was the ex-boyfriend. His eyes drifted to Kendra. If anything she looked annoyed, but Joe hadn't been given the task of analyzing her.

Shannon began speaking passionately about the new strides in metamaterials. While she seemed slightly socially awkward, her wide arm movements conveyed emotional expression. He focused on the DARPA review team to look for subtle, unconscious behavior. Thus far, all the reviewers seemed equally interested but with a cynical hesitation, evident by the way they narrowed their eyes as Shannon waved them on to the next room.

Kendra held back and practically ran to Joe. "Wyatt, I'd like you to meet my fiancé, Lee Benson."

Wyatt's eyes flicked to Joe's as he shook his hand once, then the man turned back to Kendra. "I brought you a gift." He pulled out a jewelry box.

Joe almost laughed. The man didn't bother with common niceties. In fact, there was no room for Joe to even say "nice to meet you." He might as well have worn a sign that read I Am Here to Win Audrey Clark Back.

Kendra paled and stared at the jewelry box. "Wyatt, I'm engaged now."

"Yes, you told me." Wyatt held out the box, clearly unoffended. "It's to thank you for allowing me to visit and see your lab."

The interchange managed to silence the rest of the working staff in the room. Many of them flashed sideglances to see what would happen next. "I'm sure you don't want to miss any of the tour," Joe offered, trying to change the subject.

"I'd rather have a tour from the principal investigator herself," Wyatt answered, not looking away from Kendra. "Aren't you going to open it?"

Kendra had never looked so uncomfortable. She flipped open the top of the velvet box to reveal two

bumpy metallic objects, one in the shape of a microscope and another the shape of a wheel. "Oh, thank you."

"Aren't you going to try them on?" His eyes sparkled.

"Maybe another time. I already have earrings on."

Wyatt reared back. "You know they aren't really earrings, right?"

Her eyes widened. "No? I've seen the nonmatching
thing as a style lately."

He frowned. "You still have the tree, right? The one
you add to every year?"

Joe's senses heightened. "She has so many trees, who
can keep up? You'll never meet a scientist who loves
Christmas as much as Audrey. Shall we join the tour? If
we go now I'm sure we won't have missed much." Now
the staff was openly listening.

"You know what these ornaments are made of,
right?" Wyatt persisted, his eyes narrowing.

"Of course," Kendra answered. "But I am thinking
of changing some of my traditions, now that I'm getting married."

Smooth answer.

Wyatt tilted his head. "Humor me, will you?"

She shook her head and laughed. "It's obviously part
of a computer."

He raised his eyebrows and straightened. "They're
made from circuit boards. I can see through the window
you still have the circuit-board tree in your office. You
love that thing. You brag about having specially made
ornaments every year." He shook his head. "Are you
feeling yourself?"

The tour group had stepped back inside and overheard Wyatt's last words. The tension in the room increased tenfold.

Kendra leaned forward. "If you must know, I hardly slept a wink preparing for today, Wyatt."

"An all-nighter. You've done a thousand of those." He crossed his arms. "Remind me. Where did we meet?"

Kendra pursed her lips and leaned forward. "You are here as a guest. As you can see, I have more important matters to deal with today. So either join the tour group or see yourself out."

He raised his hands in surrender. "Fair enough. I think I'll come back another day when I can talk to the Audrey Clark I remember." Wyatt looked around and nodded at lab techs and the review team, who were crossing to the other side room for the second portion of the tour.

Kendra handed the box to Joe. "Well, that could've gone better."

He wasn't about to disagree. Everyone in the room now had reason to suspect something was off about Audrey Clark. They followed the tour group into the next room. One of the scientists from the team ignored Shannon's dialogue and turned to face them. "If it's possible, I would like to stay on a little longer than my colleagues and observe the day-to-day workings of your lab."

To Kendra's credit, she remained impassive. "I'll see if I can work something out, but it might take a few days to get back to you. If you don't have that kind of flexibility, I'm afraid it won't be possible."

He raised an eyebrow but nodded. The rest of the tour went off without a hitch and the DARPA group left without fanfare. Kendra walked back to her office and stepped out with the tray of cookies. "As promised, my famous gingerbread cookies. You should know that my fiancé decorated them, though."

Joe laughed and offered to take the tray from her in the doorway. He leaned over and whispered, "Why don't you let me pass them out while you start wiping the computer?"

"You're under the mistletoe," a lab tech pointed out, a wide grin on her face.

Joe rolled his eyes upward, and to his horror, spotted the poisonous green sprig. Kendra raised her hands. "You guys know how much I love Christmas, but this probably isn't the time."

Joe placed a hand on her back and faced the group as if they were in solidarity, but the staff eyed Kendra suspiciously. Her words needed to hold more enthusiasm. Audrey had warned him. He needed to help Kendra seem authentic, so he whispered into her ear, "Just a small peck."

As she turned, wide-eyed, to face him, her eyes drifted to his lips. Joe's heart jumped into overdrive. He leaned forward and she responded by tilting her chin upward ever so slightly.

The room exploded. The sound of breaking glass accompanied a loud boom. Screams erupted behind them and the lights flickered off. Joe instinctively lifted his arms, flicking away the tray of cookies and covered Kendra, who had also hunched over.

Emergency lighting, dim, flickered to life along the baseboards. A horrible stench filled the room but Joe didn't risk looking over his shoulder to figure out what exploded. They were in a room filled with chemicals. The fumes alone might have deadly consequences.

SEVEN

That was close. Too close. And Kendra wasn't even thinking about the almost-kiss—she tucked that little moment away to obsess about later. The emergency lighting reflected off a thick slab of glass from the fluorescent fixtures embedded deep into the drywall beside her head. Another inch and it could've...

The lab door swung open, and the extra light illuminated the smoke gathering at the ceiling. "Everyone out. Leave everything!" Shannon yelled.

A hiss sounded as ceiling sprinklers deployed, spitting water on Kendra's face. She didn't try to cover her face from the water, though, because the explosion might have contained toxic fumes that could affect her skin later. Hopefully the water would wash away everything.

Kendra kicked open the office door.

"We have to get out of here!" Joe said, then bent over and coughed.

"Go! Make sure everyone gets out. I'll be right behind you." Kendra couldn't let go of the timing of the bomb. It could be a distraction to steal the research.

She should've followed her instincts and secured the research the moment they'd entered the lab. She jostled the key chain Audrey had given her that included personal car keys, an apartment key and, most important, the keys to the hard drive. The office held no backup light system, though. Kendra held up the keys to her eyes and fumbled with them. She leaned over and tried to make sense of the lock, but she'd never used this type of lock before.

Joe came up behind her. "I have one like this." His hand clumsily grabbed the keys from her. A moment later he freed the hard drive from the bolt as rivulets of water ran down the sides of his face.

"Now the laptop and all these papers."

Another boom sounded, this time from a different chemical hood. Joe shook his head. "No time!" He grabbed her hand and tugged.

Kendra pulled back.

"Nothing is worth your life. Try not to breathe until we get out." His eyes made it clear he wasn't going to stand for another second. Kendra allowed him to lead this time, as he pulled her through two sets of doors into the hallway. They kept their heads down low, following all the techs out into the fresh air.

Joe slipped the small black hard drive into the deep pocket of her Christmas blazer. At least the outfit had one good use.

Sirens sounded. There had to be a fire station less than a mile away given the reaction time. Techs in lab coats gathered together, wet and shaking with fear. The DARPA team had only made it as far as the parking lot. They looked past the techs with confused expressions, except for the scientist who had asked to stay. Kendra turned to see what they were looking at, but didn't see any smoke coming out of the main building. "Joe," she said.

"I noticed. He doesn't seem surprised. We need to find out more about him, but first I should make sure everyone got out." Kendra approached Shannon at the outskirts of the main group.

"I already know what you're going to ask. I counted. All here."

A few of the techs gave her an odd look but didn't move to open up the circle or speak to her. Either they were in shock or they knew she wasn't Audrey. Both options increased the need for expediency. She returned to where Joe waited. "At least we have the hard drive, but we need to get back inside the lab to secure the laptop."

"Aside from the office still standing, I couldn't see through the smoke enough to know the extent of the damage." He placed a hand on her back and pulled her close, as if comforting her the way a fiancé would. "The fire department and police will be all over this place today. And, if we don't want to be scrutinized by police, I suggest we leave now. With all the chaos, hopefully they don't notice you're missing for a little while."

She exhaled. "The Wyatt situation. Did you notice how everyone had questions in their eyes after he left?"

"Everyone likes drama. Let's hope that's all it was."

The fire truck pulled up front. The staff scattered to make way. Joe put a hand on the back of her shoulder and led her to the corner of the building, as if to just rest for a moment. As soon as all eyes were off them, he gave her elbow a slight tug. They slipped around the corner. "I think it would be wise to assume that everyone thinks something is off about you." He pointed in the direction he wanted them to go.

She almost rolled her eyes at the way he phrased that. "In other words, assume the Pirate already knows Kendra Parker shut down his communication network, compromised his best behavioral analyst and looks like a dead ringer for Audrey Clark." Her shoes clicked over the red tiles on the path. "If there's a chance they're trying to kill me, it's best if we get away from the campus, away from the students. Best-case scenario, law enforcement will want to talk to us but we won't know who to trust."

"For the moment, I think we should avoid going back to Audrey's apartment, at least for now. I scoped out the area maps last night. There are some places within walking distance where we could lay low for a while."

"Do you still have Visa gift cards if we need to stay in a hotel?"

"It might be wise to just focus on today."

"In other words, we're broke."

"Not exactly, but I'm also not thrilled with our finances if we find ourselves permanently on the run."

"We can't think about anything permanent. Not yet. We need to secure the research before facing that."

"At least you secured the biggest piece of the puzzle." Joe eyed her jacket pocket, where the hard drive rested, and led them north. "Audrey made it clear the rest of the research isn't worth anything without that drive."

In the light of day, Kendra would've wanted to take the time to appreciate much of the Spanish Renaissance theme present in the older parts of the campus. For the most part, they stayed in the shadows, constantly looking over their shoulders and above, in case someone was watching from one of the towering buildings, but the courtyards and reflecting pools beckoned her to stop and rest, to sit in the sunshine.

Still, she pressed on, for ten more minutes, until they reached an open-air mall. The moisture from the sprinklers had soaked through the blazer and she'd started to shiver. Joe suggested they stop in a local clothing store.

She grabbed the first normal navy sweater, pair of jeans and jean jacket she could find. Joe picked a green pullover shirt, but claimed his jeans weren't that wet, and they were out of the shop in dry clothes within ten minutes. They bundled the wet clothes in the shopping bag and Joe took a turn carrying the hard drive in his pocket.

They walked past a coffee shop. Window art wishing them "Happy Holidays" covered the tinted windows. The cartoon drawing reminded her of the mistletoe at Audrey's office. Her sister would certainly hear from her about that! Although, it was possible one of her staff had hung it up when they'd heard her fiancé was visiting.

Kendra's heart never fluttered when she'd needed to hold her old partner's hand on missions. Even when they had to kiss each other, she felt nothing but sisterly affection, although they'd only shared a peck on the cheek. Mistletoe had never made its way into an operation before.

Joe turned around and motioned to the coffee shop. "I think we should wait indoors and figure out our next steps."

Kendra followed him inside but positioned herself at

the entrance, leaning against the faux brick wall, as if waiting for someone, so she could keep a lookout while Joe went to the counter to order. He wandered over to the couple taking the table nearest to the window. She had no idea what they talked about, but within minutes they were thanking him and switching to a table farther inside the store.

He waved her over. "Our drinks are coming. Hope you're still okay with plain coffee. We have a good vantage point here to see if anyone is coming."

She took a chair and positioned it diagonally for a better angle. "What did you say to those people?"

He shrugged. "I told them my wife was learning to cope with agoraphobia, but it would be easier to have the window seat. No matter what they decided, I offered to prepay for their order as a way of apologizing for my intrusion."

This was why Joe had been promoted faster than most in the FBI. He thought out of the box and had a firm grasp of human nature and behavior. "Explains why they thanked you for kicking them out of their seats."

He shrugged. "Everyone likes to feel like a hero. So maybe you could act a little nervous if they look over."

"I don't have to fake that today."

He frowned. "If it were anyone else, I would expect that what just happened would be traumatic, but you don't have that reputation. Kendra, sometimes this type of work gets to even seasoned…" He let his voice trail off as a couple of women entered the café. "I'm trying to ask if you're okay."

Kendra hesitated to answer even though she'd basically opened the door for him to pry. Joe had a gentle way about him, but she knew for a fact it didn't stem from weakness. There was a deep strength under his control. She recognized it back at the academy because she'd seen it in herself. But now...

Her hands shook ever so slightly. "I'm weary, like this constant exhaustion deep in my bones that I can't seem to shake."

"Well, we did have a sleepless—"

"No. Wyatt, at least, got that part right. I may not be in academia, but Audrey and I apparently have that in common—we've had our fair share of sleepless nights and know how to navigate them. This goes deeper." A young man in an apron rushed over with two plain coffees and left just as fast. Kendra wrapped both hands around the cup, savoring the warmth. "At first I thought it was a normal part of recovering from my gunshot wound in that mission gone wrong I told you about, but I don't think that's it."

Joe leaned forward, his kind eyes set on hers. "Don't discount the trauma. Like you said, you were shot and woke up to find you'd been operated on. Add the double blow of remembering you'd just met a twin, who you found out took your place. That's a lot to deal with. Fast-forward to today. Your partner is transferring so you won't be working with him anymore. You've found your biological mother only to—"

"Yes." Her eyes burned. "I know." It was a mistake to bring it up, after all. Hearing him summarize the past few months stirred up emotions she needed to bury, not have resurface. The overriding feeling of utter failure crashed over her. It was as if she were trapped between a rock and high tide, as massive waves kept coming, relentlessly, preventing her from catching her breath before sinking down into the water again.

She'd lost her focus, her motivation to be the best agent. She used to be the one calling the shots on missions, the one her handler relied on the most. Ever since she'd met Audrey, other people were making arrests that should've been hers. "I think I'm just off my game."

Joe's hand inched forward toward hers, then he apparently changed his mind. He straightened slightly. "I'd like to pray for you."

At any other point in her life, if someone had asked her when she felt closest to God, she'd have pointed to time alone. Solitude had been hers for the taking for the past six weeks during her leave of absence, yet she felt farther from Him than ever. There was no way Joe, the poster boy of being close to God lately, would understand that. "You don't need my permission to pray for me. Do it on your own time, though. I need you to stay in analysis mode instead of pastor mode if we're going to survive this mission."

Joe blinked rapidly but didn't reply. Kendra seemed to bristle every time he mentioned transitioning to a pastoral role soon, but he didn't understand why. She had claimed to be a believer on day one of the academy. The FBI had welcomed them to training by showing them the badges and leftover gear of agents who had died on the clock. It was one thing to be mentally prepared for the potential sacrifice in serving your country, but to see and touch the items left behind while the speakers played the voice of an agent dying, calling for backup...

The moment had served its purpose. Many dropped training that day to return to their normal lives. Kendra and Joe, though, had shared a hot cocoa in the lounge that night, and shared their faith. He wondered now if her time in the field had hardened her heart. She wouldn't be the first.

"Does the scientist we noticed on the DARPA review team match your profile of the Pirate?" she asked.

He took a sip of the hot coffee to regain focus. "I didn't really have enough interaction with him to know for sure."

"What do you know about the Pirate? What is he motivated by?"

"Money—"

"Of course, but don't you think it has to be more than that?"

"The impression Beverly gave me was a man who discovered he was excellent at manipulating people to get what he wanted, someone who had a great deal of pride that he could run an entire criminal organization within law enforcement without risk of being identified. My biggest fear is he or she has learned more from Beverly than the other way around."

"You're saying the Pirate got even better at manipulating people because of Beverly?"

He shrugged. "A possible, though unintentional, side effect of her deep cover. Our line of work seems to be a never-ending balancing act of justification. We violate privacy because it helps stop terrorist attacks. We deceive others about our true identities because if we don't, we put a target on ourselves and loved ones. Everything we do is for security and justice, in the hopes that we are making the world a better place."

"When I was making arrests I *knew* I was making a difference." She said it bitterly, as if it would never happen again.

He nodded. "I might not have done the physical arrests, but I felt pride in my work."

"Is that the real reason you're leaving the FBI? You can't justify it anymore?"

A hiss of bus brakes sounded nearby. Joe stood as if saved by the bell. He didn't think that played a part in his decisions, but if he was honest, he wasn't entirely sure. Either way, it sounded like a topic to think on when he wasn't worried about being killed. "I think we should catch that bus."

Kendra hustled after him out the door. They boarded the bus in silence and found a seat away from prying ears.

"Beverly hypothesized that he got into government work with the intention of recruiting other agents for his own goals from the very start."

"You would think a recruiter would've picked up on that."

Joe shook his head. "It's not the job of a recruiter to worry about motivation or loyalties. They don't need to be concerned about whether or not they're hiring a double agent."

"Beyond their pay grade?"

"I'm not sure that's why, but in any case, it's the office of security who gets to tackle those possibilities." Darkness seemed to settle on her face, perhaps because his statement made her think of her double-agent father. "Obviously, there are flaws in our system."

"Obviously." She stared off into space.

Joe sat in silence for a moment, trying to think of anything else that might help. "Beverly once mentioned the Pirate likes the idea of making the world a level playing field."

"So there's a twisted philosophical reason driving him? Great. I'd much rather go after someone motivated by the money."

"A level playing field…" He looked out the window. "Maybe that's what the explosion in the lab was about… Perhaps it wasn't so much about taking us out, but more about making it easier for someone to get in."

She crossed her arms and leaned back. "I didn't get a look at the extent of the damage, but if the goal was to kill me, it was a pretty sloppy attempt."

"Well, we don't know what kind of toxins resulted from the fumes—"

"Joe, we were drenched in water within seconds, and we both seem to be breathing fine." She frowned and looked out the window. "I'm giving you a lot of latitude. How about you tell me where this bus is taking us?"

"If the online information is up-to-date, there is a station a few stops down the line that has lockers. I checked while you were still in the dressing room."

Her eyes lit up. "You want me to store the hard drive there?"

"Do you have a better idea?"

She worried her lip. "Not following typical undercover protocol, for one." She leaned back in the chair.

"If the Pirate doesn't already know our typical procedures, he'll have someone on his roster that does, right?"

He understood her reasoning for hesitation, but they didn't have much choice. "Perhaps, but are we going to throw out all our other options as well—gym lockers, a post-office box… We need to get that drive somewhere safe, somewhere not on your person."

It was as if she wasn't listening to him. She stared ahead. "If the lab incident was entirely about killing me, the Pirate would've tried harder. You were on the right track earlier. I can feel it. I think he was making sure no one else would be in the lab to make their job of stealing easier, which means we need to beat them to it." She grabbed his wrist and her eyes widened. "We need to get back to campus at the first sign of darkness."

Looking into her eyes proved mesmerizing, maybe because he could do so without any awkwardness. It was as if she was looking through him, her thoughts racing. "You're back," he said.

She flushed and turned forward. "Maybe I needed to talk more than I realized."

"Or maybe you needed prayer." He said it without thinking.

She turned slowly this time, and when their eyes met his stomach grew hot. Joe had never worked with a partner. He'd been part of a team before, but he'd never worked one-on-one with someone where they relied on each other.

"Maybe I did," she said with a slow nod. She inhaled and faced forward. "Let's skip the bus station. I have a better idea."

"Oh?"

She grinned, fire in her eyes. "Let's just say I hope you have a few more of those Visa gift cards. We're going to need a few things...and a lot of coffee. When's the last time you've been on a stakeout, Joe?"

"Never. I didn't train with the SSGs." The FBI's Special Surveillance Group was the best at stakeouts.

"Thankfully, I did a stint with them. It's a good thing you love to learn new things." She stood and rang for the bus to stop. "We've only got a few hours before you'll need to put what I'm about to tell you into practice."

EIGHT

The darkness in the lab office felt heavy, like scarves draped around her neck, tightening as she strained her eyes. The horrible smell of charred electronic components—and who knew what else—prompted the feeling. Every fiber of her tensed muscles wanted to jump up and run out. Kendra took a deep breath. It was a mission. Simply thinking that phrase helped her compartmentalize and focus. She adjusted her jacket so she wasn't sitting on an uncomfortable button.

"What was that?" Joe whispered into her earpiece.

She'd wanted to purchase the more expensive headset with a better microphone to prevent environmental interference, but Joe had opted for the cheaper set since the two-way radios were pricey. "It's just my microphone working too well." She rolled her eyes.

"I saw that."

She stuck out her tongue and crossed her eyes, knowing full well she looked childish, if he was still watching her with the night-vision goggles.

Despite the heavy caffeine load, they'd been on the move all afternoon and into early evening. After a sleepless night, the stress was taking its toll. Now, they sat still, in the darkness. Despite the horrid smell, her body really wanted to pass out. Moving around, even if only facially, helped her stay awake.

"Saw that, too."

"Good to know the goggles work so well."

"If they didn't, I'd be asleep by now. Do you want a turn using them?"

Two exhausted agents didn't bode well for a night of stakeout. The price of the night-vision goggles meant they only had enough for one set. So Kendra chose to be stationed in the office, underneath one of the counters, so she could keep her eyes on the computer station but still be in plain sight of Joe. He hid in the middle of the lab, able to see both entrances with the night-vision goggles.

The office door had been locked with a physical lock when they'd arrived an hour ago, as the smart card readers no longer worked, likely because the electricity to the lab had been turned off, which worked to their advantage. The lock proved easy enough to pick and she left the door propped open.

The lab equipment in the attached rooms had been covered in thick, white tarps, but it appeared the fire and smoke had been limited to the immediate area near the fume hoods. Audrey would, no doubt, be relieved, though she probably wouldn't appreciate the irony of their cover about the lab being remodeled coming true.

She fought back a yawn. "We could take turns sleeping," she said. "We have no way of knowing if we'll have visitors at one or four in the morning. Or at all."

"True." His yawn came through the earpiece. "Knock

it off. Your yawns are contagious. How about you take the first shift of shut-eye? The caffeine is still working on me."

Kendra shrugged but didn't reply. She did let herself close her eyes as her shoulders released a tension she didn't realize she was carrying. Except the moment she let her head tilt back against the wall, the image of Beverly's house filled her mind. She could see the side explode again, as she relived slamming to the floor, and her eyes flashed open.

"That was a fast nap."

"Did I actually fall asleep?" Her heart raced. It was hard work to keep her mind from thinking about Beverly.

"If you did, you only slept thirty seconds."

She groaned and leaned forward. The ornaments on the miniature tree perched on top of the wraparound counter jingled from the movement, as if mocking her for the mistake that blew her cover earlier. At least, she felt pretty certain her cover as Audrey was busted. "Who has this many Christmas trees, anyway?"

She scooted over so any movements she made wouldn't jostle the tree next time. If she needed to sneak up on someone, she didn't want to give advance notice.

"You can never really know everything about a person and we had very little time to brief," Joe said, instinctively knowing her real frustration. "If it wasn't about the tree it would've been something about the university they met at or the work Audrey was doing. The mission parameters were never supposed to involve someone who knew her that well."

Except, it was her sister. Even if she had only known

Audrey for a few months, weren't twins supposed to have an invisible bond?

"What made you hate Christmas, anyway?" he asked. "I'm just curious."

"*Hate* is a strong word. *Ambivalence* is more like it. I mean I never got all crazy about it like some, you know that."

She couldn't see him nod, but given the silence, she imagined he did. Joe had asked her when they were in the academy why she was the only one not moping about missing holiday traditions like some of the other cadets in training. She smiled at the memory because it had become clear he had just wanted an excuse to complain about missing his own family's tree trimming. He also had to be one of the few men in the world who genuinely enjoyed putting up Christmas lights.

"And," she added, "once I started working covert ops I missed a lot of holidays, even during the probationary years." She thought about Audrey, and the way her face beamed over the decorations, the movies, the cookies and even the clothes. "Maybe I just haven't given myself permission to try to enjoy it as an adult."

"I hope you get a chance to at least try when this is over."

"Me, too," Kendra said softly. Audrey and Lee planned to get married this Christmas. The idea boggled her mind, but she wanted to be happy for them. She wanted to tell her family and beg them to be there despite the super short notice. They would instantly know she'd been keeping the revelation of a twin from them for the past few months. You couldn't get away with anything but 100 percent honesty in her family of cops. How could there be a family celebration, though, if the Pirate was still out there? And if they did somehow get out of this she would be forced to tell Audrey about meeting their real mother… She took a deep breath, and the darkness and whispers they shared emboldened her. "Tell me more about Beverly."

He didn't answer right away and the silence frustrated her. Making the request made her feel vulnerable enough. But maybe in the dark, if she heard more, the uncomfortable insecurity that'd plagued her ever since she'd met Audrey would disappear back into the shadows, where it belonged.

"I'm not sure what to say. I don't feel like I really got to know the real Beverly very well."

"Better than I did." The longing and disappointment in her voice came through strong enough to make her cringe. She really had a problem with controlling her tongue around Joe. He seemed to make her emotional defenses go on the fritz.

A door creaked in the distance. They both went silent without another word. Kendra popped up into a crouch and waited. Ten seconds dragged on as she ignored her body's protest at the uncomfortable position. Her ears strained for any more sounds. Her own soft breaths sounded loud in comparison. She took a slow inhale and held it for a few more seconds, listening.

Perhaps she'd misinterpreted the situation. Maybe Joe had been the one to make something creak, or it was just a security guard passing by. They'd both noticed when they'd sneaked into the lab that the security cameras at the points of entrance were no longer working. Her knees started to object in the crouched position as she spent a few more minutes of silence with no light, no indicators of anything happening.

What if Joe had fallen asleep in the quiet?

Two small taps sounded in her earpiece.

Kendra's neck tingled with awareness. The sound was Joe's prearranged signal that two people were coming. He would've spoken up and told her if it was just interference by now, and with his goggles, he'd have noticed she was in pounce mode.

A beam of light moved in her peripheral vision through the glass panel above Audrey's desk. The lab areas had sealed doors without any windows to the outside. The absence of light had prevented her eyes from seeing even the slightest of shapes until now. She squinted, trying to make out the shapes past the doorway, as well. Had they seen Joe? The store-bought night-vision goggles would be no match against a military-grade flashlight beam.

It hit her all at once that if her eyes had adjusted, then the same would be true for whoever was about to enter the office. Especially if he carried his own flashlight. There was nowhere to hide in the small office except...

"Stay here and keep watch." A male voice sounded muffled and far away in her left ear, but louder and crackling in her right. So the voice was closest to Joe and his microphone then. One thud came through the earpiece. Joe's tap on the microphone meant one person was headed her way, confirming the voice she'd heard.

The tap also meant she only had a second before someone entered, likely with a flashlight. Kendra needed to move and couldn't afford to make any sound. She pushed off with her left foot and slid underneath the counter space until she reached the empty spot behind the door.

The location was no guarantee that someone wouldn't see her, but it at least gave her a fighting chance. She didn't see a way to surprise her opponent if she had to crawl out of a hiding place, though.

She stayed hunched over, not allowing even her head to press up against the underside of the counter. Her hair snagged on the rough unfinished particleboard with the slightest of movements. She let her right knee hit the floor to create a gap, ignoring the way her left ankle protested at the awkward positioning.

Footsteps approached.

She pulled her weapon out of her holster but held it behind her back.

The light beam swept across the floor in front of her. She held her breath and slowly pulled her weapon higher, ready to aim if she needed to. Finally, she was about to meet the Pirate and put an end to Masked once and for all.

Joe lifted the night-vision goggles off his eyes but kept them on his forehead. If the flashlight beam hit the lens, they'd be useless, anyway. He peeked around the edge of the workstation. One person remained at the threshold between the adjoining rooms as a lookout.

Joe placed the goggles back on and twisted to look around the other side of the workstation, where he could see Kendra, except she was no longer there. The tall figure stopped at the doorway. Joe's heart jumped into his throat. They were without a team, without sufficient data, and he had never planned or participated in a stakeout before. This was already going wrong on an epic level.

If the person entering the office spotted Kendra—even if she managed to subdue him—the other person would be alerted. If the intruders did have guns, both he and Kendra were without tactical vests.

He should've never let Kendra talk him into this. When he was alone and praying, he felt peace about dying whenever his time might come. But now, in the midst of danger, he wasn't ready. He still had so much he wanted to say and do.

Mere minutes ago, he'd wanted to share what was on his mind about Beverly, but he also knew, with such an emotional topic, that less than 10 percent of what the other person heard would be from the actual words. If he was going to help her understand what he knew about her biological mom, he needed to do it face-to-face to make sure she was really hearing the intended message.

He faced the back wall and took a deep breath. There was no more time to examine all the options. He popped up into a squat. The man shined his light in the office, focused on the portion of the desk with the computer and files. So far nothing was heard over the two-way so the intruder had yet to see Kendra. How that was possible, Joe wasn't sure. It was a tiny box of an office with barely enough maneuvering room for one.

The lookout, clad in a mask, twisted and swung the flashlight beam into the vast adjoining room, which was filled with machinery. The only way Joe would be available to help Kendra was if he took out the lookout first. Joe sprinted forward, keeping his eyes on the dark shape in front of him as his target. He felt his shoes crunch on debris, but he couldn't afford to look down. The figure began to turn, the flashlight beam twisting as well, on its way to spotting him.

His fingers itched to pick up the gun at his back, but he refused to grab it if they were unarmed. He didn't want to aim and point if he had no intention of actually pulling the trigger. Not again. If he pointed and a threat was in front of him, his training kicked into hypervigilant mode and he'd likely take the shot. For now, he'd focus on taking out the light source. He grabbed the top of the microscope on his left and, using the momentum of his run, tossed it in the direction of the flashlight.

Kendra inched forward ever so slightly. The intruder in the office appeared to have a man's build, judging by the breadth of the shoulders. A ski mask covered the entirety of his head, but that worked in her favor, as it would muffle sounds slightly, but she would eventually need it off to see his face.

He held something with two long handles as he made his way to the computer station. The beam glinted off the office window again to reveal a bolt cutter in his hands. He moved to cut the cables attached to the hard drive and the computer to the locks. Too bad for him, Kendra had already switched computers with one of the other stations and planted a fake hard drive in order to be sure he'd be baited fully inside the office.

She grinned. Time to discover the Pirate's identity. She slid her left foot diagonally out for balance and carefully twisted until she was crouched behind the man. He'd already cut free the hard drive and was working on the cable for the laptop. She straightened slowly and aimed at his back. She resisted the impulse to spout some sort of pirate-themed banter, like "All hands on deck." Best to keep things professional.

A female's cry sounded so loud in her ear that Kendra forced her focus on her gun instead of ripping out the offending earpiece. Pinging metal and crackling glass followed in her earpiece. What was going on? Was Joe hurt?

The man looked up at the noise and caught Kendra's reflection in the window.

"Hands up," she said. "We need to be properly introduced. FBI Spe—"

He spun so fast she almost missed the bolt cutter swinging right for her side. She twisted and moved her right hand to block it, but as the metal hit her forearm she buckled and almost dropped the gun. He dropped the bolt cutter as he lifted his foot and his kick aimed for her solar plexus.

Kendra dropped to her knees, barely able to see straight as her arm throbbed, radiating pain all the way up to her spine. His leg grazed the top of her head with another kick. "I said freeze," she shouted with gritted teeth. She used her left arm and punched the side of his other thigh with as much force as she could muster.

He grunted and grabbed the laptop, thrusting it forcefully at her face. She leaned back, slamming into the open door, and momentarily felt trapped. She realized her tactical mistake instantly as he twisted the laptop and slammed it into the side of her head. She heard herself scream, without intending to, as she dropped to the ground and covered her head.

The pain blinded her...or maybe it was the lack of

light. The flashlight beam had gone dark, but she felt the man jump over her and into the lab.

"Watch out," she called out for Joe's benefit, forgetting that she was probably shouting into his earpiece. She forced herself to standing before running after the man.

She tried to catch up as he darted into the adjoining room. A discarded flashlight rested on the ground, illuminating a covered piece of machinery the size of a commercial grill. It reflected enough for her eyes to adjust. Joe held someone's hands behind their back with one hand and had placed his gun between their shoulder blades, though his finger was nowhere near the trigger. The man was running his way, the laptop in one hand and held high as if he planned to use it as a weapon again.

Joe whirled around, forcing the other figure in the ski mask to face the oncoming threat. Except the eyes in the ski mask widened and the figure dove forward, blond hair sticking out of the mask, despite Joe's hold on the hands, now leaving Joe exposed.

Kendra cried out, too far away to stop the man as he struck Joe's head with a tactical flashlight instead of the laptop. Joe groaned and dropped to the ground.

The man and his freed accomplice wasted no time running to the door. Kendra yelled the command to stop again. She couldn't shoot them. She had no justification for deadly force, and she needed the Pirate alive to take down Masked. She raised her weapon and, taking inspiration from the earlier explosion in the lab, aimed at the set of fluorescent lights, despite being turned off, nearest the exit.

She pulled the trigger and a heartbeat later the shattered tubes rained down, but the two figures bent over and continued until they rushed through the side door and disappeared. Kendra ran forward. Joe hadn't moved from his spot on the ground, but thankfully, the glass hadn't touched him.

"Joe?" She touched his face. He was unconscious. An impact to the head could be so intense the brain actually hits against the skull and shuts down, hopefully only for a moment. She knew from experience. Except, in her case when it'd happened, she had needed surgery to survive.

She slid her fingers to the spot underneath his chin. *Please let me find his heartbeat.*

NINE

Joe groaned, his hands cradling the spot where his head throbbed, and he opened one eye. He'd moved one second too late. "Sorry. Was I out long?" He dragged a hand down the side of his face. "I took a bat to the brain, didn't I? I thought my head was going to snap off for a home run."

She exhaled and laughed, her voice shaking. "You're alive."

He felt his eyes widen. "Was that under question?" If he looked that bad in the dark, it must've been a hard hit.

"The point is you're going to be okay. You might have some trauma to get checked out, though, so stay down. I'll be back. I can't let them escape." She jumped up. Only then did Joe smell the telltale scent of gunpowder. Glass bits littered the floor in places he didn't remember before. Kendra didn't wait for a response and ran off, glass crunching under her feet, until she disappeared. But he could still hear her and the huffs of breath coming through his earpiece.

Joe lifted his left leg and wrapped his hands underneath his knee. Forcing his leg down while maintaining his hold allowed him to use the momentum to lift himself to an upright sitting position without much effort. He groaned aloud at the sudden throbbing of his head from the shift, though.

"You're still there?" Kendra asked. Her voice was a whisper. "Are you okay?"

The radios were equipped to go up to four miles of range, supposedly, provided there weren't significant geographic obstacles in their way, but he didn't want to test the limits. He couldn't allow Kendra to go on her own. His mandate was to keep her safe. Now more than ever they needed the Pirate's identity before the vast network of Masked rallied against them, or Joe and Kendra might as well say goodbye to their futures now.

Kendra's breathing grew more rapid. "They're leapfrogging me."

Joe stood up even though his equilibrium hadn't fully returned. Leapfrogging—that was a surveillance tactic where operatives were told ahead of time that their target was coming. But how could that be possible if it was just two people who had run out? Unless…

"There was a backup team waiting outside? How many?"

"Apparently. I don't know."

She released a high-pitched screech and something resembling rocks clattering against metal reverberated over the microphone. Her voice was hushed. "I'm hiding. Joe—" She pulled in a sharp gasp. "Silencers."

Now that did fit the modus operandi of the Pirate. He never drew attention to himself and would do whatever it took to take care of business as discreetly as possible. Joe gripped his gun tightly and ran out the front exit instead of following Kendra, as would be expected.

He didn't know the campus as well as Kendra, seeing as she had visited Audrey a few times, but he had studied a map Audrey had available in her apartment the previous night. The temperature had reached the sixties by late afternoon, but now, in the middle of the night, the cool air had a bite to it. Not quite freezing, but it couldn't be more than a ten-degree difference.

His stability increased as he ran, though his right ear rang slightly. Good thing the earpiece was in his left. He darted behind some foliage and gained his bearings. "Where are you now?"

She was panting. "On the move again. I'm not sure how many. They were standing guard, waiting for the two in the lab, but then two more—"

"Where? We'll worry about how many when I reach you." He felt his blood pressure rise and his head began to warn of a tension headache, most likely aided by the knock to the head.

"I—" He heard her footsteps slapping on what sounded like one of the tiled sidewalks connecting buildings. "There are so many arches on this campus."

He almost groaned aloud. The architecture was beautiful but repetitive. "Those are everywhere. I need something more." The sound of water rushing reached his ears.

"The fountain?"

"Just past. Behind the library."

The tall futuristic building was the main library. He could see it. "I'm on my way. Any students? Security guards?"

"No. Not yet. I'm trying to get off campus."

"Good." If she was past the library, she was leading them far away from the student housing. If he remembered his map right, she'd be in between a grouping of various geological, chemistry and biological laboratories.

He took off running. A quiet but distinct ping sounded and gravel rock flew up in his face. He ran down a set of stairs, then darted behind a massive rock. Except many of the smaller rocks started to move. Joe feared he'd lost his senses from the head trauma until he remembered Caltech's famed Turtle Pond. He held his breath and stared at them a half a second longer to make sure he was operating on all cylinders. Sure enough the rocks were turtles. Since he didn't want to risk their lives, either, he needed to keep moving.

He slipped through a grove of trees and another ping sounded. Two leaves rained down over his head and he found the set of arches closest to the library and fountain. He hid behind one and breathed hard. So far he hadn't seen where the shots were even coming from. "They're good at hiding."

"Yes." Her voice crackled. The monstrous library probably counted as a geological disturbance for the radio signal, although who knew what possible interferences were within the many labs peppered throughout the campus. "This feels choreographed, Joe."

The warning twisted his stomach. They were better at this than he was, obviously. He belonged behind a desk, not dodging bullets to save the day. He might as well have been asked to lift a thousand-pound weight without tools to get her to safety. This wasn't in his wheelhouse. Maybe a better man would embrace the challenge to save the day. Not him. He had to question, overthink and overanalyze everything.

A shadow in his peripheral vision moved. He started sprinting and felt dirt kick at his heels. He kept pumping his arms, darting and weaving between the crooked trees that seemingly sprang up from the ground. His throat burned like fire and his ears roared from the intense sprint.

He crouched behind a cement edging that held a raised pond filled with lily pads. The soft sound of frogs croaking barely masked his heavy breathing.

"I think they're trying to corner me." Kendra's voice sounded strong and confident, but Joe knew better. No one felt good about being trapped. "Are you still with me?"

"Yes." If he was right about their respective locations, he needed to get past one more corridor to catch up to Kendra from around the back of the chemical lab, as long as one of the shooters didn't take him down first. His blood pumped hotter instead of cooling down from his brief respite.

Beverly had acted as if she'd somehow been training him while he was unaware the last several weeks. But really, what did Beverly do except encourage his hyperobservant tendencies and his need to please others? While Kendra wanted to be the one making arrests—she admitted that herself at the coffee shop—he would choose to change the world behind the scenes.

He would rather be the guy behind the chair than the hero. Maybe that was the real reason he'd never gotten the girl—it was a new thought he could save and analyze on another day. Footsteps sounded at nine o'clock and three o'clock, approaching fast, reminding him that Kendra couldn't do this alone. He supposed that was what mattered. He pulled out his gun.

Kendra sneaked a look through two branches thick with leaves. The top of a man's head poked out from behind a tall pillar approximately fifty feet away. The other shooter she couldn't get eyes on. She held her gun in her hand but her fingers quivered in an uncontrolled manner, so she didn't dare use it yet. The men had silencers. She didn't. Besides, one shot would draw attention to her location and she wasn't clear on just how many gunmen were out there.

The old Kendra would've shot back without hesitation. The last time she'd been in a shooting match, she'd killed a man but had also been shot herself and on the surgery table for hours. The recovery was relatively minor given that the alternative was death, but she hadn't hesitated in using her gun again when she went in to be tested at the range. Fear hadn't entered the equation back then.

What if her pride hadn't pushed her forward to take on a gunman by herself back then? Maybe she wouldn't have been shot. And what about now? She'd left Joe behind to go after the Pirate by herself because she thought it was her only option. Except maybe her pride had blinded her then, too.

"On—" the radio crackled to life and cut out "—notice—off—think—" She wasn't even getting every other word of what Joe was trying to tell her. It was useless. "—meet—"

Another shooter rounded the corner and placed a hand to his ear. The shooters had their own system of communication. They *were* practicing the leapfrog surveillance technique, but it seemed they'd lost her. Although, if Joe suddenly showed up, she'd be spotted. She didn't want to think just how many armed men with silencers were out there. Beverly's warning rang truer than ever. If Kendra called for backup, she wouldn't know whom to trust.

The shooter out in the open turned his back to her. Kendra slipped out of her hiding place and ran to the back of the building, where there were even more arches and a structure that looked like a cement gazebo. From there, it would be a dart across the street and she'd be off campus, with access to numerous buildings and houses and, hopefully, escape.

The whoosh of a bullet soaring over her head made her drop to a crouch, but as she did, she spotted Joe thirty feet away huddled behind a matching pillar. "Joe, nine o'clock," she said. She repeated it in a hushed voice three times fast, hoping that despite the static interference something would get through.

He turned in the opposite direction, looking across the street, as if trying to get his bearings first, then he spun in her direction, his gun raised. His eyes widened with recognition. He pointed with his free hand to the street. They were in agreement, but they had no cover. Behind him, a man rounded the corner. It was now or never. She sprinted across the road. Joe matched her speed as they converged together. He held his gun behind him, waving it wildly until they reached the cover of a low-hanging tree.

"Look behind you," Joe said.

A man approached from behind Joe.

"There's one behind you, too." There was nowhere to run except right into the tall brick building awaiting a remodel that had caution tape surrounding it. They hurdled over the tape and ran into the unlocked front door of the building. Joe slammed the door shut behind him and flipped a lock.

Darkness once again greeted them. Without any light to guide her, she was forced to flick on her phone. She fought back a cough as the dust irritated her already burning lungs. "Let's run through the back door and lose them."

She took the lead and ran across the lobby, which was littered with chunks of drywall. No wonder it was being remodeled. As soon as the back door was directly in her sights, she flipped off the phone and reached out for the door handle that should be right in front of her. Joe's footsteps behind her emboldened her. She pulled open the door only to see a man six feet away, lifting his weapon to aim.

Joe's hand covered hers as he slammed the door shut and locked it, as well.

"How?" The wobble in her voice revealed her frustration. "They couldn't have known we would go in here."

"You said yourself they were leapfrogging you."

"Even so, there's no way someone could've beat us to that back exit. They would've had to get to the side street and then the alley to get behind this building. They couldn't have moved that fast!"

Joe answered with a grunt. "Those doors are pretty

solid, but I wouldn't put it past them to get through it. Let's head upstairs and get a good vantage point. We can see how many we have to deal with."

He flipped on his own phone, but kept it low and led them down a long hallway. They both were out of breath, and while they no longer sprinted, they kept up a fast pace. Rooms lined both sides, but they were missing the doors. "Why don't I see windows?"

Joe flicked his phone light to the side. Wood covered the rectangle where the window should've been. "Oh, this is not good. Sometimes they sell everything they think can get them a buck before working on a place."

He moved the beam upward. The place really was in a state of disrepair. Insulation hung down from the ceiling in strings and sections. Joe put away his gun and reached for her free hand. "I'd hate to think that was asbestos. Come on. Maybe there are some intact windows upstairs."

She didn't need his fingers to pull her forward but the contact had an odd, calming effect she'd never experienced during a pursuit, or in this case, a retreat. "I still don't know how they managed to corner me like that." She tilted her head. "And what was with all that wild gun-waving back there? Since when do you look like a shooting maniac?"

Joe used precise control whenever he handled a gun. After all, she'd never be able to forget the way he'd saved her life.

"I was testing a theory."

He pressed open a remaining door that still held a "stairway" sign. He let go as they jogged their way up to the third floor, as the second floor wouldn't give them enough advantage in height.

"What theory?"

"Did you notice how little they actually shot at us?"

"Like me, they didn't want to risk being heard and drawing attention. Especially true on a college campus. If the police had come, you know we'd have no one from the FBI able to back us up. We'd be sitting targets."

He turned back to her, the light emphasizing his frown. "They all had suppressors."

She almost rolled her eyes as it took her half a second to know what he was talking about. An analyst always made a point of using correct terminology, while the public, and even some agents, such as herself, called them silencers. "The ones that actually took a shot, yes. I'm not sure exactly how many were out there."

He stopped at the platform to the third floor. "What do the suppressors tell you?"

This time she did roll her eyes. "That they didn't want to be heard."

"What else?"

Oh, if there was one thing that grated on her about analysts, it was when they thought they had the answers. They either berated you or led you down a path of questions until you arrived at the same conclusion. Since she wasn't part of their training, she didn't know if it was an annoying personality trait they shared or a technique to keep hotheaded agents from going rogue on a mission. "Joe, spill it."

"One second." He turned away and stepped in the corridor. Once again there were no windows that hadn't already been boarded. He groaned and turned to her. "This really isn't good."

Her blood started to boil. Failure was not an option. They needed to get safely out of here, away from the men, so they could regroup with a better plan. "So we figure out how to remove a section or something." She strode purposefully past him and toward the window, but the floor gave out. A scream escaped as her left foot dropped into nothingness. She flung her arms up into the air and dropped her gun, as her hands searched, desperately reaching for something to save her from a dark descent.

TEN

Joe lunged, his phone flying from his hand as he grabbed her upper arms before they disappeared. He stepped backward, pulling, but she worked against him, twisting and working her shoulders as if trying to climb up through the air. "Stop flailing," he said through clenched teeth, but he knew it would be almost impossible.

Confident he had her right arm secure in his hand, he briefly let go of her left one. She screamed but he reached down and wrapped his left arm around her waist instead. He inhaled and lifted upward, making sure she was free of the jagged bits the hole had created before taking a step backward.

"I would never let you go," he said. Her body relaxed ever so slightly as he stepped back until they both reached sturdy footing again. At least, he thought it was sturdy until he felt his right heel begin to sink.

He shoved Kendra to the left, hoping she wouldn't go down with him.

"Joe!"

He fell backward and thankfully only his heel had

gone halfway through the floorboard. Kendra looked at him with wide eyes from her position on her hands and knees. Joe's discarded phone's light pointed at a ceiling panel, this one disturbingly concave.

"Termites?" she whispered.

"Best not to think about right now." He grunted and scooted backward, taking one breath to close his eyes and lift up a silent prayer. *Please guide our hands and feet safely out of here.* He opened his eyes and nodded at Kendra. "Hallway. Now. You first."

She crawled, slowly, testing each movement tentatively before moving forward. He continued a similar journey with an odd crab-walk of sorts, moving backward, and came across her gun and his phone along the way.

She crossed the threshold of the room. Still on her hands and knees, she made it to the hallway. "It feels firmer," she whispered. "You're almost there."

He made it over the threshold and felt the change instantly, as well. A deep weariness in his bones begged him to lay prostrate on the floor, but if he stopped now he felt certain he wouldn't move the rest of the night. Or maybe ever, if the Pirate's cohorts reached him first.

Kendra stood and brushed little bits of debris from her pants.

His throat ached, exhausted from the constant tightness of the day. What he wouldn't give for an ice-cold bottle of water. He wanted to inhale deeply, but after what he'd witnessed, he pulled the collar of his shirt up over his mouth to act as a filter before he did. Kendra followed suit. "Maybe we should go back down."

"Anywhere but here." Joe stood and handed over

her gun as his chin gestured to go back to the stairway. "At least the stairway seems to have stone or concrete framing, but the walls don't look great so I don't know."

They stepped in the stairway and she faced him. "Before we go anywhere, what were you trying to get at earlier?"

He hesitated. He didn't have time to reflect on his theories before making a logical analysis. He wanted a thoughtful dialogue without leading her to the same conclusion in order to see what theories she came up with. After all, she had much more experience in these types of scenarios.

"Joe?"

It was clear she had no patience for such a dialogue. "I have this assumption in my head that shooters who use suppressors are typically—"

"Sharpshooters?"

He shrugged. "They at least know their weapons and can shoot well."

"You're aren't saying they missed on purpose, are you?"

"I find it curious. At least in my case, they chased me but only actually shot at me twice—once at the tree leaves and once in the gravel. Both places won't leave a mark or an obvious bullet hole."

She frowned. "Mine was a little closer than that but only two shots, as well."

"You said yourself that it all seemed choreographed. As if they already had this backup plan in the event you showed up."

"You think we were expected?"

"I think *you* might've been. I think you were right

that the planned explosion in the lab wasn't meant to kill you. However, that was likely set up before anyone suspected you weren't Audrey Clark."

"After my cover was blown, they had time to figure out how to kill me. Then why did they miss if we're following that line of thinking?"

"We're dealing with the most cautious criminal Beverly has ever encountered. It's like he's playing four games of chess at once." Except the Pirate wasn't working alone. He had a roster of traitor agents or criminals at his beck and call. Not exactly a fair match of wits and certainly not playing by the rules.

She blinked. "If he approaches it like chess he's thinking about all the possible moves we might be making."

He exhaled. "Multiple steps ahead of us, even, and he's planning his defense."

"The communication segment we took down had an intricate amount of layers and lieutenants before Lee and Audrey reached the CEO of the thing. If we're really dealing with the person that created and organized the network, then we have every reason to believe he's got his bases covered." Her shoulders dropped. "But it also means we're up against a genius, someone much smarter than us."

"Hey, speak for yourself." He was kidding, trying to alleviate the hopelessness he currently felt, but Kendra didn't crack a smile, either. "What we know for sure is only two people entered the lab and the person left keeping watch was—aside from the tactical flashlight—an unarmed woman." He held up his hands. "I'm not trying to make any statement on gender, but I do wonder if the Pirate had been expecting both of us to be there, if he wouldn't have planned the lab break-in a little differently."

She pursed her lips. "I don't know for sure if the man in the office had a gun. I don't think he did."

"So in the event *you* were a planned complication, it's only logical to reason they had a plan to take you out."

"Except you seemed to think they didn't want to shoot me."

"According to Beverly, the Pirate would want you taken care of in a way that could never remotely lead anywhere near him. If we met him this morning, he'd have good reason to worry. When I waved my gun like a madman back there, no one took a shot. It was as if they were more scared that I might shoot at them, which might create some evidence that could lead to them."

Her chin jerked to the left. "This building…"

He nodded encouragingly. Now she was tracking with his thought process.

She met his gaze, eyes wide. "It's a pile of rubble ready to come crashing down, isn't it? You think they herded me—us—here?"

"I think it's a possibility. Let's check the rest of the building, quickly. If this was there backup plan for if you showed up, there might be something here that's worse than taking our risks with the gunmen out there."

She nodded and blinked rapidly. "Let's stay in the hallways, though. I don't want a repeat of what just happened."

He almost reached out to grab her hand. He didn't want a repeat, either, but he wasn't sure he could forget what it felt like to hold her in his arms. He meant what he'd said about never letting her go, but something in his heart had changed, as if he wasn't sure the sentiment ended at her safety. More than likely the exhaustion was playing on his vulnerable state.

They rushed through the hallways as a team, shining lights into alternate rooms, searching for any hidden dangers and possible windows. The third, fourth, fifth and sixth floors were clear of both. Without windows, the fortress of brick started to feel more like a prison. "That leaves the first floor," he said. "We never really examined it."

She nodded and gulped. They exited the stairway with guns ready, in case any gunmen decided to join them. The rooms leading up to the lobby, where both the front and back doors were located, held nothing. The hallway past it was all that was left to be explored.

At the last room something reflected off his phone beam. He peeked inside. There was a collection of odd items lining the inside wall: seemingly empty two-liter bottles that held brown stains, bottles of pills, coffee filters with shiny white-looking crystals on them, a few bent-up frying pans and a propane tank. He took a step back as Kendra looked over her shoulder.

"We have to get out of here," she said.

"Is it a bomb?"

She shook her head. "No. It looks to me like just enough paraphernalia to frame a federal agent on leave for trying to start a meth lab."

Framed? That didn't exactly seem like the Pirate's usual methods. It would risk Kendra finding an ally in another agent and tracking down the Pirate's identity. No, he usually left the evidence to be found after they were dead. Something clicked in his brain and he ran for the lobby. He heard her footsteps behind him. "The front door. When I locked it there was something taped next to it I didn't take time to read."

He slid to a stop at the metal door and pointed his flashlight at the paper taped to the brick wall. His mouth went dry as he read the words. "It's a signed permit for demolition to happen in just a few hours. There's probably a copy posted on the outside of the building, too."

A strangled cry of frustration escaped Kendra's lips. "That's why the sloppy attempt at a frame. Under a pile of rubble, no one would question it. They'd see chemicals and two dead rogue agents and write it off as natural consequences for our drug-making ways." She shook her head. "Joe, we need to take our chances and find a way out of here." She held up her gun. "I think it's the only way. Are you ready?"

Joe closed his eyes for a second. Was it the only way? Before he could find a moment's peace, she flipped the bolt and pushed.

Her head snapped forward and back with the effort. "It won't budge!" She turned and ran for the back door.

"Kendra, wait up. Let's plan."

Except she'd already flipped the bolt open to the back door with the same result. She spun around. "Something is keeping these doors shut from the outside."

Of course. They'd probably been boarded shut for public safety and only removed for a short period to lure them inside. The gunmen likely placed the locks back on while they were upstairs searching. "I think it's time to call someone. Maybe your old partner? If you trust Lee, maybe he could call someone he trusts that's close enough to help. It's risky, but I can't think of any other option at the moment."

"It's exactly what Beverly told us not to do."

"I think she also didn't want us to die."

Kendra placed her hands on her hips and paced back and forth. "Okay. Fine. Yes, let's do it."

Joe lifted his phone screen and clicked the phone option, but he noticed the line through the tower symbol. Dread seeped into his bones. "Kendra, is your phone working?"

Her eyebrows jumped. "Are you kidding me?" She pulled out her phone and fisted it. "No signal. We really are trapped, aren't we?"

Kendra wanted out. It seemed like the walls were closing in the longer they were there. The dust was thick enough to write a message, but leaving behind a list of suspects with their dying breath wouldn't do any good if the building was scheduled to crash down around them.

She needed to take a deep breath without feeling like she'd choke. She wanted to see more than what the light from a pitiful phone beam could provide. "The roof."

He pointed the beam down the hall. "Good idea."

Fresh air and the possibility of a phone signal pushed her into a run for the stairway. Besides, it could provide the vantage point they so desperately needed. Her pace slowed the higher they climbed. When the stairs ended at the top, she turned the doorknob. Locked. The discouragement was almost enough to make her cry, the most unprofessional outpouring of emotion she could exhibit. She needed to get a grip. She blew out a breath.

"I'm not trained in this, but may I try?" Joe said. She

frowned and stepped aside. He took out one of the few remaining prepaid credit cards and slid it through the space of the door and swiped downward.

Nothing happened.

He pressed his left shoulder into the door, turned the knob with his left hand and tried again with his right. A small click.

"You just earned a lock-picking certificate in my book."

He smiled as he stepped back and opened the door. Clean air—well, as clean as Pasadena could get—drifted down a small, open stairway that led to a flat roof. Kendra sucked in a deep breath in relief and ran toward the stars above. She glanced at her phone before she stepped on the sticky tar. "I still don't have a signal. How can that be?"

Joe looked solemn, despite the success of reaching the roof. "If I were the Pirate planning our demise, I'd utilize a signal jammer so others didn't ruin my plans." He lifted his phone. "No signal here, either. I don't think this is a coincidence. We're not getting a call out."

Of course there would be a signal jammer. The Pirate had been one step ahead of her the entire time, just like the Masked Network had been for the past few years before Audrey and Lee finally had success. She hunched her shoulders and stayed low as she made her way to the edge. She heard the telltale whoosh of a suppressed bullet hitting a century-old palm tree on the west side of the building. She dropped down. "They're letting us know they're still watching us."

Joe nodded. He peeked over the opposite side of the building, then quickly sank down to sit. "I don't think they saw me, but there's someone stationed at the back exit of the alley. They've covered all possible escape routes." He turned off his phone. "You should turn off your phone and save the battery. We can try again when morning gets closer."

She powered down the phone and put it in her pocket. "Morning?" She crossed over and sank down beside him, leaning her head against the half-brick wall. "Are you that ready to give up?"

"Kendra, I'm not used to this. I've gone forty-eight hours without sleep and I literally cannot function one second longer. I'm not ready to give up, but I think if I had just fifteen minutes to close my eyes, I'd be a lot more use."

"You also had quite a bump to the head," she admitted. "Fine. Take a little shut-eye, but I'm not letting you sleep the night away." She shivered, whether from the cold or the frustration she wasn't sure. Joe noticed. He reached his arm around her shoulder, but she could tell he was fighting the chill, as well.

"I'm sorry I don't have a coat to offer you," he said. "But I'd rather be up here in the fresh air than risk breathing in asbestos or who knows what else down there. I think we should try to get as comfortable and warm as we can, given the situation. Besides, I find when you slow down, sometimes the answer comes to you."

She agreed, since she didn't have a better idea. Kendra leaned into him, eager for warmth…and comfort, but she wasn't ready to admit the latter. He wrapped both his arms around her and leaned the back of his head against the brick wall.

Her eyes adjusted to the light that the stars and sliver

of moon provided. Sure would've been nice if there'd been a rope or something useful left on the roof. Not so much as a TV antenna or satellite had been left behind. "If they took everything to sell, why did they leave those sheet metal doors?"

"They can retrieve those after demolition," he said sleepily, his eyes still closed. "It's for safety to keep people out—ironically."

She stared at his peaceful face as frustration built. "I'm not sure I can rest for a second without knowing what our plan is going to be."

He breathed in deeply. "I know. I'm praying."

Praying for a plan or praying that she could rest without knowing what the plan was? She didn't ask, but she really wanted it to be the first option. His eyebrows furrowed ever so slightly. When life got hard, people often would say they were praying about something, but Joe was one of the few people she believed when he said it. Whereas when she was growing up, she'd see her mom and friends gather at different church events and many of the ladies would inevitably ask for prayer about something. Her mom would nod and never mention it again.

As an adult now, she knew logically that she couldn't see the state of her mother's heart, but she also couldn't ever remember her mother ever praying with her, either. And on the odd occasion one of Kendra's church acquaintances in school had ever asked for prayer, Kendra would agree but rarely remembered to do so except the odd quick lifted-up thought at the time of the request. Did that even count? Maybe. But the result was that she didn't ever share her own prayer requests with anyone because she doubted they'd actually do it. And if they weren't going to do it, then wasn't she just whining about her troubles? Or was that just an excuse her pesky pride relied on?

Ever since she'd found out about Audrey, she'd become more closed off from others than ever. It probably was odd that she hadn't told her parents yet that she'd found a twin, wasn't it? They didn't even know she'd been shot or had surgery or taken a leave of absence. She'd chalked it up to the covert operative lifestyle, but it rang hollow now. "Is pride a result of jealousy or constant competition?" The question tumbled out of her mouth, but she wasn't sure she wanted an answer. "Is it hereditary?"

Joe breathed in slowly. He opened his eyes and turned to her. "I suppose it could be all those things to some extent."

The warmth his arms brought seemed to open the reins around her heart. "I've always been in competition with someone," she admitted. "Sometimes I wonder if I'm hardwired for it. My parents—my adoptive parents—never gave me any reason to worry about their love. I mean, I was their only daughter. They made a point of always telling me that they *chose* me." Her eyes stung but she blinked back the pain, embracing it even. "I liked hearing it, but apparently it didn't matter. I still had to prove to everyone—to myself maybe—that I deserved a place in the family. My dad was a policeman. My mom was a former policewoman. One by one, my brothers joined the force, and each time, my parents told me that it was their choice and they held no expectations. So what did I do? I became a federal agent. You know why?" She looked over to find Joe's eyes wide, searching her face.

"Why?"

A hollow laugh escaped. "Because I wanted to serve in law enforcement, too, but I wanted to one-up my brothers. I thought it was the equivalent of policing on a more elite, national level." The sting in her eyes increased. "So ridiculous, right?"

"Oh, I don't know. It makes sense to me." He shifted and rested his chin lightly on top of her head.

It struck her how well she fit in his arms, almost as if she was meant to rest there. Her heart quickened at the thought and she shoved it as far away as possible. "I think I've probably inherited a lot from my parents, whether I like it or not. Look at Audrey. She went into academia and became a professor, just like Beverly. I became a covert agent just like my—my father."

Her throat ached. It was hard to admit she had a father, especially since he was a murderous double agent. "I've been forced to make a lot of questionable moral decisions in my line of work all for the good of my country, but I can't imagine…" She sucked in a breath. "I mean, to pretend to love someone and then marry them, start a family, only with intentions to kill—"

"Hey." Joe's voice was husky as he gently hugged her tighter. "We don't know what it was really like for him. We don't know everything that happened."

He was right, of course. She sighed. "What I do know is Beverly eventually became a covert operative, too, so we're both like our mom one way or another. Maybe it's inescapable."

"Sure, there's plenty of things we inherit that we

can't escape, but tendencies and careers are choices. Whatever your initial motivation to become an agent, you're good at being an operative and you love it. Don't let doubts rob you of your confidence."

Her head dropped, and it felt as if he'd turned the knife she'd placed in her heart. She hadn't told anyone her dark secret yet. "I'm not an operative anymore." Saying the words aloud hurt even more.

His grip slackened as he sat up straight. "What?"

ELEVEN

The despair Joe had felt in his bones suddenly dissipated. "Did you quit the Bureau? What happened?" The woman in front of him wasn't merely exhausted. She looked beaten.

"After I was shot and my handler found out I had a twin, he pulled me off all my undercover cases. My cover, Mrs. Kimmet, was rumored to have trusted the wrong person and disappeared. Mr. Kimmet—Lee, my partner—went back to play the part of the grieving husband and close any money-laundering cases he could. The other agents posing as aides and clerks at our shell law firm are taking care of the rest and shutting it down." She looked up at him. "None of my family knows. I haven't told anyone yet."

"Lee doesn't know you're off covert operations?"

"No. He knew Mrs. Kimmet could no longer exist for Audrey's safety." She stared ahead, her voice measured and monotone. "Since Lee and I were no longer partners, he wasn't briefed about my next assignment. As soon as I was cleared for work after I was shot, I got the news that I would be working a desk job. I thought it was temporary until my handler made it clear it was permanent. I decided to take my extended leave of absence then and there."

Lee tried to imagine Kendra behind a desk and failed. "I'm sorry. That sounds like a lot to process."

She shrugged. "I let Lee and Audrey believe I was going off the grid for the sole purpose of looking for my biological mom. The truth was I sat around in my apartment for two weeks before I decided to actually go after her. Tracking down leads gave me purpose, at least. I've been in covert ops for so long, playing the part of a fake lawyer who helps criminals money-launder, that lately I'm not sure who I am anymore. And no one is going to hand me a file with another persona to play, so I better figure it out fast."

"You need time to process and not just about your job. You were presented with a twin by surprise. Your biological mom is a spy. That's a lot handed to you in a short time, and then there's the little drama of someone trying to kill us." The wind stilled for a moment and the slightest scent of sulfur and exhaust fumes mixed in with the fresh air. Breathing in the good with the bad served as a reminder. He didn't know if they were going to survive until tomorrow or not, so maybe now was the time to tell her his thoughts on Beverly. "Do you ever wonder if Beverly picked the families who adopted you on purpose, as a way of connecting with you?"

She turned suddenly, looking up into his eyes. "What do you mean?"

"Well, like you said, Beverly is most at home in academia. Audrey was placed in a family with two professors. And you… You were placed with two law-enforce—"

"What?" Kendra twisted fully, out of his arms, her face animated. "You think she got to choose where we went?" She stared at her hands. "That might explain how the adoption agencies in both Michigan and Montana conveniently lost the records. One was by fire." She shook her head. "I hope Beverly didn't go that far, but if she was worried about us being discovered and kidnapped…"

Joe didn't want to get her hopes up that Beverly had put that much thought into where she placed the twins. "I don't know. But what I do know is Beverly is a genius. She wouldn't have survived this long if she wasn't, which leads me to suspect…" He shrugged. "She probably did."

Kendra smiled softly. She looked radiant when she smiled. Just as fast as it appeared, it disappeared. "Well, that's almost worse because why couldn't she have figured out how to have a relationship with us while we grew up if she's so smart? Or, maybe she's not as smart as you perceived. Either way, she thought we could do this, and we failed."

"When I met Beverly in church…" He searched for the right words. "She might claim, after the fact, that her sob story was all a ploy to win me as an asset or apprentice, but I recognized a crisis of faith when I saw one. Beverly was seeking God's help to make her relationship right with Him and right with you. And if Beverly is to be believed that I'm a good analyst, then I believe that she really was wrestling with those things."

"How can you be sure it was authentic?"

"Because I recognized the desperation in myself." He shook his head. "I was struggling—still am to some extent."

"Why?"

He hesitated. It was easy to be vulnerable in Kendra's presence, but he wasn't sure he was ready to discuss it with anyone yet. Though, this might be their last night alive so it might be the best time. "I'd only been an associate pastor for a couple weeks, and I was already burned out. It has to be some kind of record. I was doubting my decision."

Kendra tilted her head and studied him. "Tell me straight up. Why did you decide to do it then?"

"Become a pastor?" That was a loaded question. "The short answer is it wasn't a knee-jerk reaction. I took two years of online and weekend classes to earn my Master of Divinity."

"Yes, but you're always taking some new class online or in person. When we met you told me your hobby was college." She laughed. "Who says that?"

He mirrored her smile. While not the easiest subject for him right now, he was glad to see the change in focus had helped her. "I like school. Guilty."

"So what made the hobby lead to a new career?"

"Well, I've never told anyone but since this seems to be a night of firsts—"

"And possibly lasts," she said softly.

"I haven't given up, Kendra. We're not alone in this." Though he would admit he'd never been up against a bleaker situation than this. "I need to trust that He's with us or I won't be of any use to you or anyone else."

He sighed. "The trusting is actually the answer to your question."

She frowned. "How's that?"

"During my service in Afghanistan, there was a group coming in for a humanitarian effort. We were tasked with checking out the surrounding buildings to make sure it was secure before they arrived. I was in an abandoned building. I looked out the window and had an intense need to drop to my knees and pray."

He shook his head because he suddenly felt like it was yesterday. "I've never felt it as strongly before or since. I tried to think away the urge. I can pray just as easily standing up. But I felt I needed to humble myself and drop to my knees. Right then. Despite feeling foolish, even though there was no one in that room but me, I kneeled." Simply talking about it brought the memory and feelings to the forefront of his mind. His throat swelled with gratitude yet again.

"Okay…" Kendra moved her hand in a roundabout motion, encouraging him to get on with the story.

"The moment I hit my knees a rocket-propelled grenade soared over my head."

Kendra gasped. "Right where you were standing?"

He nodded, glad he didn't need to explain in more detail. It gave him a moment to tap down the surge of emotion. "I was spared. In fact, no one died that day. But I was the only one who got a neon sign telling me I was spared for a reason. And right or wrong, I do battle with a sense of constant pressure to make sure my life is worth something. I'm still trying to figure out the best path to do that."

"You were making a difference as an analyst."

"Thank you. I know I was, but I also burned out fast there."

"That surprises me. You seemed to enjoy analyses of all types."

She was right. He did. "I suppose I got tired of always looking for the bad in people."

Her mouth opened in surprise for a moment before she smiled. "I suppose I'm guilty of the same thing. I can understand that."

"There's also a part of me that's still searching for *which* thing I was saved for, the purpose. Even though I know more than most that He doesn't necessarily work that way." Joe blinked rapidly. This really was starting to feel like the last night of their lives. He'd never admitted his darkest fears to anyone, let alone himself. "I'm in my thirties, and I still don't know what I want to do with my life." He shook his head. "Wow. That's really messed up, isn't it?"

She laughed. "Wanting to please God but struggling how to do it? How to best use your gifts and talents? I'm pretty sure that's called being human." She smiled in a way that made him feel like their hearts had a direct link to each other. She closed her eyes and leaned her head against his shoulder. "Thank you for sharing with me. I know it wasn't easy. You're like me—you keep things close." Her hand slid down his arm and squeezed his hand. "You mentioned praying. I think I'm ready to do that together."

He tried not to flinch at her touch or express surprise at her change of heart. It was as if she'd thrown off her armor. Joe could see that girl he met at the academy again. His heart beat faster. Why could they be vulnerable with each other so easily? He returned his focus to above and closed his eyes. "Father, thank You for keeping us safe. We're desperate for Your wisdom and courage right now..."

Her head grew heavy on his shoulder. He opened his eyes and looked down. Kendra was sound asleep against him. Ironic that he was the one begging for sleep minutes ago, but she'd been the one to fall asleep. He fought against laughter, lest he wake her. He remained still but wide-awake from all the revelations and renewed sense of purpose.

He wasn't officially retired as an analyst, after all, and they weren't dead yet. Perhaps he needed to pretend he had all the FBI team members at his disposal. If he imagined an operation with that advantage and thought about what his coworkers would say and do, maybe he could discover some new insight, some new ideas.

Once her breathing grew heavier, he moved to gently hold her head and lower her to the ground. Time was running out. He'd asked for wisdom, and with the new burst of energy, he felt the need to seek it wholeheartedly. The alternative was to sleep and accept death in the morning.

Kendra ran to the edge of the roof. No escape there. She ran to the opposite edge, but the roof shrunk in size by several feet. How could that happen? When she turned around the roof continued growing smaller in front of her eyes. Sirens approached from all directions, but they wouldn't reach her in time. Joe appeared and placed his hand on her shoulder. "I would never let you go."

She tilted her head. He'd said that to her before, hadn't he?

"Kendra!" He shouted her name as she began to feel the tremors of an earthquake.

Her eyes flashed open to find Joe in her face, his hand shaking her shoulder. She recoiled and hit the back of her head against the back ledge. Her heart pounded furiously. The telltale beeping sound of a truck backing up must have been the sirens she'd heard in her dream.

An odd chanting and a voice shouting through what sounded like a megaphone fought against approaching growls of big machine engines. She pressed through the fog of sleep and sat up, shivering. The sky had lightened, but the sun must've still been on the horizon as it wasn't bright yet. "What time is it?" Her teeth chattered. The more she woke up, the more violently her muscles shook. "I didn't think it'd be so cold in California."

"Just after seven in the morning. It's not December in the Midwest, but it's still chilly."

"I didn't mean to fall asleep." Nausea threatened to send her to the edge of the roof. She'd slept away all the time they'd had to figure out a solution. She stared forward at the brick wall—if only she could will it to have an invisible ladder for them to climb down.

"It's okay." He paled. "I didn't mean to, but I fell asleep for a few seconds, too. I think. I'm not sure. Over fifty hours without sleep, I think I unintentionally blanked out for a few minutes, or I would've woken you sooner." He held up his phone. "If I was awake I would've turned it off. It's almost dead now."

She contorted in an odd stretch, trying to relieve the

knot underneath her left shoulder blade. It was hard to think straight with all the noise. "What's the shouting?"

He grinned. "A protest. People gathered to protest the demolition of this building. I believe it'll help our chance at escape."

She felt her cheeks flush as she remembered her dream. What if she'd said something aloud? The voice through the megaphone grew louder. Someone shouted about needing more housing, not more mansions. "If there are protestors, maybe we could wave and get their attention." She moved to take off her shoe. "I could throw something to—"

"I already thought of that. Well, not the shoe specifically. Listen to the machines warming up and the shouting. No one is going to hear us. We're up six floors high. No one is looking up here."

"That's why we throw something. We have to at least try!"

"Analyze the possibilities. Say we managed to get someone's attention, and they in turn were able to get the demolition crew to stop the machines long enough to listen. If they happen to see the tops of our heads, the police will be notified and discover us. They want to ask us a lot of questions, and there's the little matter of the meth lab on the first floor."

"We would look guilty and wouldn't know who to trust. I'm fully aware." She rubbed her eyes to clear the rest of the sleep from her thoughts, but the shivering had yet to stop. "And the Pirate would still find a way to take care of us, to keep us quiet, especially since we still don't know who he is."

"If we have another chance for escape, shouldn't we

try that first?" Joe reached for her hand. "Stay low. Let's get inside the building and get you moving. It's now or never."

She crouched and every bruise she'd acquired in the past day protested. "Now or never to do what?"

His eyebrows dipped and somehow made his narrowed eyes look even bluer. "They can legally start demolishing in about ten minutes. Now or never to get out of here or we'll go down with the building." He took her by the hand and led her down the stairway.

"I don't understand. How do the protesters help us escape?"

He continued to hold her hand. Only this time it didn't bother her, like when he'd tried to take charge earlier. The thought rattled her, especially after her dream, but she supposed the warmth and steady support he offered was the difference.

"Timing is everything." He glanced back, his entire face animated. "As you can tell, the protesters provide plenty of noise and distraction, once we get down. I evaluated the whole building. The northwestern corner is the only spot where the men guarding the alley and the front wouldn't be able to see us."

She frowned and tried to remember what area around the building looked like, but it had been dark when they'd run toward it. "Because of trees?"

They reached the fifth floor and Joe stopped outside of a room. "A palm tree is right on the western corner, where the fence and a lot of vines obscure sight to the building." He held up his phone and shined the beam on the covered window. "We knock this out and should find a fire escape."

"Really? You think they just never noticed a fire escape?"

A chagrined expression crossed his face. "It might be generous to assume it's in working order. I didn't dare shine a flashlight on it from the roof, but I think even if it's bare-bones we can still make it work."

Hope blossomed and suddenly the cold didn't matter. "But once we get down?"

"The protesters were in the street, which means—"

This time it was sirens instead of beeping that seeped through the brick walls. "They're blocking traffic. The police will come to help and ensure citizens stay safe while the demolition occurs."

He nodded, clearly proud of himself. "If there's even two cops on the right side of the law, our turned agents, hired guns or whoever they are won't want to draw attention, right?" Joe gestured forward. "I tested the floor earlier. We should be okay, but stay alert."

The sound of people chanting grew louder and the cranking of more than one construction engine was unmistakable. Joe looked over his shoulder. "I think we're running out of time. Are you on board?"

"What about once we're on the ground? What then?" The questions rushed from her mouth. She felt like she was flying blind. There'd been plenty of times she'd run first and made decisions based on instinct, but that was when she was calling the shots and had a backup team.

Joe paled. "I have an idea, but I don't think we have time to discuss it."

Did she even want to know? She tamped down the pride that wanted to demand every detail of someone else's plan before taking a step forward. If she hadn't selfishly fallen asleep then maybe she'd be the one asking him to trust her.

He searched her face. "Are you ready? Once we start on this course of action there's no turning back."

The machine sounded like it was revving up to move. Even though they were at the back of the building, once a wrecking ball hit they'd be sunk. Literally. "You're the analyst. Lead the way."

His eyes widened and he gulped. "I've never done this before." Before she could offer any advice, he took a run at the window and jumped, his leg out in a front kick. His heel missed the center of the board but made contact with the left side, precariously close to the wall.

The wood cracked open as he fell backward. Kendra lunged forward and caught his shoulders before he hit the floor fully. "No sense testing the floor again," she said with a grunt. He scrambled upright. They ran toward the board, each pushing on either side of the crack.

"Hurry!" Joe grunted as he shoved out the remaining side of his board. Kendra managed to push hers out enough that surely they would have enough room to get out. She looked down to find the rusted-out frame of what *used* to be a rickety fire escape. Maybe thirty years ago it could've actually been considered a working one. He was right about the palm tree, though. One side of the trunk brushed against the corner of the set of stairs that led down to the next platform.

Kendra stuck her head out the open window and looked up. Above them the palm fronds looked heavy and hung down precariously. She'd heard that each one weighed upward of a hundred pounds. Apparently, the cities in the area weren't in agreement on who should maintain the massive trees. Audrey had even pointed out a palm tree on a previous visit and said two fronds had dropped and killed a man last year.

The protesters were silent, or maybe their chants weren't loud enough to cover the deafening roar of a crane followed by a crash. Joe's wide eyes met hers. "It's started!"

He lifted a leg and hopped up and through the window. He balanced on one of the few remaining bars left on the platform. Kendra held her breath, waiting for him to fall, but he turned and reached his hands out for her. She heard the whoosh of metal and a crash. This time she felt the rumble underneath her feet.

She grabbed Joe's hand and climbed out the window to join him, though she kept a grip on the windowsill. The palm tree shook slightly from the demolition forces, as well. Moving quickly but cautiously, they slid along the remaining rusted bars to the stairway portion.

She grabbed the metal bar and gingerly took a step at a time until they reached the next platform. "Fourth floor." She took a deep breath. One floor closer to the safety of the ground, and one floor closer to men with silencers and law enforcement that couldn't be trusted. Another crash sounded. The entire building shook and rumbled, but amazingly the side didn't come crashing down yet. The bolts holding the metal to the wall, however, were wiggling their way loose. She forced herself to look away and focus on keeping her feet on the metal railing that looked the least rusty.

Joe exhaled. "So far, so good. Just keep moving and pray the building doesn't come crashing down until we have." He took another step. An ominous creak, followed by a snap, grabbed Kendra's attention. A six-foot-long-by-six-foot-wide palm frond dropped.

"Joe!" She grabbed his arm and tugged with all her might to get him out of the path as the formidable palm hit the platform just above them. She exhaled in relief. Joe looked shaken, as well. They rushed to the next set of stairs. The top platform snapped and collapsed into the stairway above them. The palm dropped to the next platform, the one they were just on.

This time Joe didn't need her urging. He jumped to the next platform. She was one step behind him, almost running into his back, as she felt the frame of the fire escape give way from the building. Whether it would be underneath a pile of rubble, a heap of rusty iron or a giant palm frond, the result would be the same. They were about to be crushed.

TWELVE

Joe turned and grabbed Kendra by the waist and lifted her up over the railing. Her surprise must have given way to understanding because her toes found the edge of the platform and her hands grabbed the outside bar. "Go," she urged. He released her and kicked his leg over the railing to join her.

"Now!" Kendra's voice was full of panic. She twisted as she jumped off.

Joe didn't take a second to look back. As soon as his other leg was over, he pushed off. The rumble grew louder from the front of the building. His right foot hit the ground but refused to take the weight. His knees hit the earth and he rolled, groaning, as the force of the impact traveled through his bones.

Clanging sounded, and he looked up to see the palm tree and metal platform slamming against each other as what little was left of the escape framework came tumbling down. The brick wall seemed to shift, as if unsteady.

"Joe!" Kendra tugged at his arm.

He flipped over and struggled to a standing position.

She held out a hand. He grabbed it and allowed her to pull, dragging him forward despite his throbbing ankle. They stepped into the alley past the northwest corner. Joe reached for his gun with his free hand. At the far end of the alley, a police car waited. An officer jumped out. "Hey! You can't be—" The officer looked up. "It's coming down! Get out of there!"

Joe looked over his shoulder. The top of the building began to collapse into itself. "The fence!" She didn't need prodding. She ran at it and grabbed the top of the wooden, vine-covered fence he'd planned for them to jump. Her foot reached the middle of the panel and she scrambled up and over. He struggled to run and his arms strained to lift himself up and over. The fence began shaking as well when he kicked over his legs. The air shifted and shoved a gust of dust at his back. The building was going down.

He dropped to the ground, his backside hitting the gravel and the back of his head hitting the wooden slats. Little rocks peppered the fence, and he didn't want to wait around for anything bigger to break past the flimsy protection.

He shoved himself up and, crouching, followed Kendra. They ran through a yard in bad need of water but completely enclosed and unseen from the street. At the back of the property, a yellow mansion, weathered and in need of repairs, sat with no signs of life at such an early hour. Kendra pumped her arms ahead of him but every few steps she reached for her gun, as if checking to see it was still ready and waiting. She coughed as she ran, and Joe prayed that they hadn't inhaled asbestos waste or anything with lead that could hurt them years from now. Though he supposed he should focus on today's murderous possibilities instead of the future.

Dust fell from his eyebrows. He brushed it away, though his eyes stung as if he'd missed some. He needed clear vision in case guard dogs suddenly approached. Kendra found the driveway leading to a gate first. Joe's ankle begged for relief, but he gritted his teeth through the pain. He needed to lead Kendra to safety. This was his plan and he needed to see it through.

At the end of the drive, a control panel held a red button that allowed people leaving the property to easily exit. She slammed her palm on it and they ran through until they reached a sidewalk. "We're on a different street," she said.

"I know. The property takes up the entire corner. Come on, before we get noticed." Construction-machine noises still reached their ears. Joe prayed the great mass of dust would hide them. The officer had been a fair distance away at the end of the alley. Even though he'd seen them, unless he'd been tipped off, there was no way he could identify them. Although, if the Pirate's crew had been listening to the police radio, they'd likely hear of two people who ran out as the building crumbled. Hopefully, they'd assume Kendra and Joe were trapped by the falling debris, and it would buy them some time.

At every property without a gate, they sneaked through to get to a different street. Kendra wanted to avoid the sidewalks, especially ones with palm trees hanging over them. "I'll never be able to look at a palm tree the same way again."

"And I'll never look at an old building the same way again," he replied.

Following as serpentine a pattern as possible, they reached the southern entrance to the campus.

Kendra placed her hands on her hips. "Why are we going back here?" she asked.

"I didn't want to argue with you about my plan, but I think the only option is to head straight to the Caltech security office and get ahold of the lab's security footage. I know it's a risk, but if we don't, we lose—"

"The only lead to potentially identify the Pirate." She nodded and brushed off her clothes. "The fire marshal and the police will be wanting to talk to Professor Audrey Clark about the explosion in the chemical lab by now, but they won't automatically consider her a criminal. First, they'll worry about her, check the hospitals..."

Joe pulled back. He had completely expected a fight. "Yes."

Kendra pointed at her face and drew an invisible circle around it. "Any dust still there?"

"You look beaut—great," he amended. There was a piece of something in her hair, though. He reached and moved to brush it away. Their eyes met as he did so and her gaze seemed to paralyze him.

"Thank you," she said softly. "For what you did back there. You saved my life...again." She blinked rapidly and averted her eyes. "For what it's worth, I'm glad you listened and dropped to your knees in Afghanistan. I can't imagine my life without having met—"

A college student sped past them on a ten-speed so closely that Joe took a step away from Kendra. His heart warmed at her words. She was trying to thank him for the difference he'd made in her life, but the back of his neck suddenly burned with shame. He was looking for some big purpose his life was supposed to fill because he'd been saved once. What hubris to assume he needed to fulfill some extraordinary career path that *he* felt was worthy of God saving him for.

The revelation took him by surprise. There was freedom in simply living his life in an honorable way and trusting God would use it for His purposes. His shoulders relaxed, and he smiled.

She raised an eyebrow. "Did I say something funny?"

"No. I think you just snapped me out of a prideful funk I think I've been stuck in for years."

She pursed her lips. He didn't expect she'd understand, but before he could say anything else she grinned. "Funny. I thought the same thing about you last night."

"Really?"

"We're not here to chat, Joe."

"Right. Security office."

"I know where it is. It's part of the parking garage on the west."

"No. According to my study of the campus maps and brochures when we were at Audrey's apartment, the security administration office is different than the security patrol office. I think we need the admin to get a release of the footage. Two different places, and thankfully for us, the administration office isn't actually on campus. It's on the street right next to it." He pointed to what looked like a farmhouse that'd been remodeled into a house from the early seventies with green shutters. "Oddly enough, security, along with parking, has been relegated to the back of the employee credit union. Should be on the left-hand side. The administrative offices should be open by now." He struggled to lead the way as his swelling foot pressed painfully against the collar of his shoe. "Do you know what you're going to say?"

She flashed him a smile. "Thanks for getting me this far, but this is a job for a covert agent. I've got this." They stepped through an opening of hedges to avoid walking around the front of the building. A stairway led to the second floor of the house. He grabbed the railing and hobbled up behind her. A gray sign with white lettering indicated he was right. Parking and Security Offices. She opened the door and pointed to a bench along the wall. "I think it'll be easier if you wait here."

"So I won't need a cover?"

"I think the only thing you need to worry about is using those analyst skills to make sure we weren't followed."

Kendra's heel dragged slightly against the green, aged carpeting leading into the administrative office. She stopped for a second to remove a piece of rock stuck in the tread of her shoes before making a beeline to the glass office that held the placard that read Security Director. She spotted a man in his late fifties wearing a red sweater over a crisp white dress shirt. He waved her inside.

"How can I help you?"

"I'm Professor Audrey Clark. I was hoping you could help me access the security footage at all possible entrances and exits of my lab at the engineering building."

He stood from his desk and walked around the corner of it. "I'm sure you know that policy dictates you must first get a signed directive from—"

She sighed. She didn't know any of the policies, but she knew how to ask for exceptions. "Of course. But you can understand that after the explosion, I have a vested interest—actually everyone on campus should—in expedience so we can prevent this from ever—"

"Whoa." His eyes widened. "*That* lab. Professor Clark? I didn't realize." He leaned against the edge of his desk with his hands crossed over his chest. "In that case, we have ourselves a predicament. As I told the fire marshal yesterday, our security footage seems to have disappeared. The hard drive allotted for those two cameras is gone."

Kendra almost groaned aloud. "Gone? How does that happen?"

"Believe me, we're looking into it. We'll enlist the police, if need be, to help."

"I should hope so. DARPA will not be happy about this. In fact, I would imagine this might make things harder for other labs to get grants if security is going to be lax."

His neck flushed a deep red. Anytime funding was at risk, the issue at hand was sure to be taken more seriously. "As I said before, Professor, we will get to the bottom of it. In all my years this has never happened. Caltech's honor code has served us well."

Ah, the famous honor code. It basically said that no member of the Caltech community would take advantage of another member. In her line of work, she couldn't imagine trusting every FBI agent within the Bureau that much. Collaboration existed but there was also an unspoken sense of competition. She would be the first to admit guilt at trying to one-up her coworkers, at least before she found out she had a twin and biological mother in the world. "Isn't it best practice to back up the security feed to a server somewhere?"

"Of course. But, as I explained to the officers, the feed went offline approximately thirty minutes before the incident in question. Except, no alerts or notifications were sent out like they're programmed to do."

"You're saying you were hacked?"

His facial expression was impassive. "I'm saying the IT guys are treating it as a top priority, but as of yet, they haven't been able to get the server back up and can't find a reason for the anomaly."

"What about archives?"

"Those, too, Professor." He shook his head. "We are cooperating with the investigation and aren't jumping to any conclusions until we have all the facts. Off the record, though, these sorts of accidents don't just happen."

The invisible burden on her shoulders tripled in size. The footage was their last hope of a lead to the Pirate. They had nothing to give Beverly—if she still was alive—and the NCS. Her throat tightened at the thought. Was it time to give up, say goodbye to her loved ones and become a ghost?

"Did the fire marshal reach you?" He tilted his head and studied her.

She glanced up, so lost in her thoughts she'd almost forgotten the man was still in the room. "What?"

"Both the marshal and the police were trying to locate you yesterday to ask some questions. Apparently, you just disappeared after the explosion." He glanced at the phone on his desk as if unsure whether he should report her now. "Are you okay?"

Kendra moved her hair back slightly, sure he'd be able to see the lump she felt growing on her temple and the grime and scratches her neck and hands bore. He would assume it was from the explosion as long as he didn't look too closely. "To be honest, no." She purposefully let her voice shake. As she hoped, his arms dropped to his sides and he relaxed, so she continued. "As you can imagine, it's been very upsetting. I did sustain a few injuries but nothing life-threatening. It's been hard to rest and recover, though, not knowing if my research or staff are safe." She feigned concern. "You don't think they think I'm a suspect?"

Compassion creased his features. "I'm sure they just need to ask you questions, as well. All standard procedure. Get in touch with them. They'll understand. They allow time for eventualities like injuries before they issue a warrant."

"A warrant?" She placed her hands on either side of her face. "I better get in touch soon. Did the fire marshal leave a card?"

He nodded and picked it up from the desk. She read the name in bold. If the fire marshal was doing his due diligence and investigating properly she might be forced to trust him. At the very least, she'd have to make clear that Audrey Clark had an alibi and was nowhere near the lab. Before Kendra disappeared off the face of the earth, she needed to make sure everyone knew Audrey wasn't implicated.

"Thank you." She spotted a small break room in the corner of with a vending machine and a refrigerator. "Could I trouble you for one more thing?"

After the surprised look on his face, she managed to

leave the security administration offices with two bottles of water and a bag of ice. Joe wasn't where she'd left him, though, as the hallway was empty.

"Over here." A whisper reached her ears.

Around the stairway, there was a small waiting area she hadn't noticed before that contained two armchairs and a coffee table, which was covered in brochures and magazines about the campus. Joe pointed to a map in front of him. "I needed to refresh my memory and the darkened windows here offer a prime—" He noticed the bottle of water and ice in her hands. "Thank you."

She took the seat next to him and gulped down her water faster than intended. The smell of dust and mold had yet to leave her sinuses fully, or maybe the memory of it had grown so strong it'd become permanent. What a horrible thought.

Joe secured the zippered bag of ice against his ankle by placing it inside his sock. The small waiting area didn't lead to anywhere but the two restrooms. It seemed like an afterthought as a way to use the space.

She sat up straight, unwilling to relax in the soft-cushioned back. "If I let myself rest, I'm scared I won't be able to get back up again."

He nodded. "What did you find out?"

"Dead end. The Pirate got to them all first." She waved the business card. "And law enforcement is looking to ask Audrey Clark questions. Apparently, I don't have much time before they request a warrant." She blew out a breath. "If we need to go off the grid, I need to make it clear Audrey has a twin before I disappear."

Joe's hung his head. "We don't have much time, then.

We have to go back to Audrey's apartment before that warrant is issued."

"What? No. We avoided it all day yesterday for a reason. That's the first place the police will look to find Audrey for questioning."

"That's the first place they likely *have* looked. How likely will they try again this morning? You said yourself they don't have a warrant yet to enter. I need to get there right away." He avoided her gaze. "I left my real driver's license in Audrey's place. It's in my go bag."

"You've got to be kidding me." A rookie mistake that Kendra had no right to scold him about. He never asked to work covertly, and he'd saved her enough times she needed to give him grace. If they were about to live the rest of their lives on the run together, there would be time to teach him everything she knew.

"It's possible Masked has already identified me as the guy who took down Beverly's guard, but if there is a chance they don't, I want to keep it that way." He exhaled. "Aren't you worried about your family? About them being used as leverage? I'm wondering if we should warn them."

"Anyone who goes after my family will regret it. I have two brothers that still live at home. Darryl is the only one who moved...three blocks away. I think it's because they're too lazy to get their own places, and Mom is a pretty good cook." She shrugged. "They say their rent is helping Mom and Dad pay off their mortgage faster. The point being that the Pirate wouldn't be so foolish as to target an entire family of police officers including the chief, right?"

Joe didn't reply but furrowed his brow.

"Joe? I'm asking you if he would risk it."

"I studied the campus a lot for possible hiding places." He pointed at the map. "There are four libraries at Caltech. All but one doesn't open until later this morning, but this one—Sherman—is open twenty-four hours a day if you have an ID to scan." He glanced up. "You still have Audrey's?"

It was still attached to the lanyard around her neck, so she pulled it out from underneath her shirt. "Yes. But why? And don't think I haven't noticed you avoided my earlier question."

"You're probably right, but I don't want to get your hopes up. The only thing I do know is the very next step to take." He tapped the map. "Our next stop is here. This library is also where they store lost and found items."

She crossed her arms, fighting back irritation. She wanted a positive answer, not a probability, but she took a look at the map. "I don't know about the found part, but I definitely feel lost."

THIRTEEN

Joe's ankle felt on fire, but this time from the extreme cold the bag of ice provided. The library stop had proved very useful to provide a disguise. "Hats suit you," he said. They emphasized her eyes, but he kept that to himself.

Kendra grimaced as they strode across campus. "Orange is not my color, and it certainly doesn't go with red." They'd found her a gray cap with the university logo in orange, and a red sweatshirt with the logo in white. With her shiny, dark hair hidden in the hat, Joe thought she'd prove unrecognizable to those looking for her. She could certainly pass as a graduate student.

He, however, had only been able to find a pale green pullover with a hole in the armpit that fit him. A knit puce cap over his head completed his makeover. "I never thought I was one for fashion, but I'll admit this ensemble is hurting my delicate sensibilities."

"There's nothing delicate about you, Joe." She smirked. "I'll be glad if we can both get our bags before we're forced to move on. I had some cash in my bag that will come in handy."

"We can't go into a ghost protocol yet. We have Audrey. She'll be able to identify everyone who was in that room. We at least have a place to start."

"Audrey didn't know everyone from DARPA or those other researchers."

"Yes, but that should be easy enough to track down. At least easy enough for someone from NCS."

"I don't want to get Audrey involved."

"She's already involved."

Kendra shook her head. "Even if I need to take a billboard out, it will be made clear I acted alone while she went on an innocent trip home. She's not to be in danger. She already did that once because of me." Her voice shook ever so slightly and Joe almost stopped right there and pulled her into his arms. "At least one of us should get a happily-ever-after." Her eyes darkened, as if making it clear the vulnerable wall had been fortified.

He exhaled. "Let's grab our stuff and figure out how to get Audrey in the clear. Once that's done we make our way back to Florida, and I'll attempt to use the same drop system I used at my hospital visits. Hopefully, we can make contact with the NCS director."

She flashed a smile. "Have I mentioned I'm glad I brought you along?"

For a second Joe believed the carefree, ambitious girl he met at the academy had returned, and they were on their way to an exercise, not one of the last stops before having to be on the run forever. He stopped at a glass door. "Walk thirty feet out in the open and you'll enter faculty housing. You still have Audrey's key?"

"Affirmative. You'll follow in a minute."

Each time they crossed an opening in between buildings, they'd taken turns traveling separately but they always maintained a visual until they reunited inside. Now, as soon as she entered the building, he would wait a little longer to make sure they weren't followed. If he didn't meet her at the apartment in the minute after that, she should assume there was a problem, grab the bags and get out.

He shifted his weight entirely to his good leg and began counting to sixty. The small break in action let his thoughts ramp up to racing again. He experienced a strong surge of thankfulness they'd escaped the demolition, but he was still confused as to why God would allow their crazy plan of escape to work—albeit barely— but didn't stop Masked from stealing the security tapes.

He felt equipped, even if he was both figuratively and literally hobbling, to be Kendra's right arm as an analyst at the moment. He also felt equipped for the pastorate. Both options left him filled with purpose yet drained emotionally.

Ironically, despite the situation, he felt most in his element in this very place. The halls of universities and colleges comforted him, as if he'd returned home. If he could converse with students and professors and learn for the rest of his life, he felt certain he'd be happy. But didn't that mean it was just an escape? Maybe it was an excuse to stay young and carefree.

Kendra's cap disappeared through the side door of the apartments. He twisted to check all angles. Other than a couple of students on bikes, he didn't spot anyone else and rushed toward the apartments himself. What if there was another reason he felt at home on this campus, one that had everything to do with whom he was with?

Joe half limped the thirty feet to the building. The hairs on the back of his neck tingled from the cool breeze. People passed by, and he tried to look casual as he checked his surroundings before opening the door.

His ankle began loosening up and didn't smart as much going up the stairs. The ice pack had helped, so if it was a sprain it must've been minor. The Christmas wreath on the second floor was a dead giveaway now that he'd seen it before. He didn't need to remember the number of the apartment. He lifted his fist to knock when the door swung open.

Kendra's face had a gray pallor, as if she was about to be sick. She didn't say anything, just grabbed his wrist and tugged him inside, closing the door so close behind him that she almost caught the back of his sweatshirt in the door.

"What's going on?"

She pointed in the direction of the living area and kitchen. Since it was an open floor plan, he only had to take one step to understand her horror. A bundled pack of bags filled with white powder sat between two people, spread out on the floor between the couch and the television. A male and female, black ski masks tossed to the side, stared at the ceiling with lifeless eyes.

Kendra paced behind the couch. The vinyl wood floor showed rough scratches, likely from dozens of careless tenants over the years and people not removing their shoes. She never removed her own shoes when she entered a house. She wanted to be able to run out fast if she needed to.

"The blonde woman worked in the lab. I remember her because I thought she looked like a stock model."

"Yeah, Audrey had mentioned her. She came highly recommended but Audrey couldn't speak to her work yet."

Kendra kept her eyes trained on everything aside from the rug past the couch. "The man, the man with the—"

"From DARPA."

"Actually I think he was the consulting scientist that asked to stay." She frowned. "Why would he ask to stay if he was the one that broke into the lab that night? Perhaps he was the one that made the explosion in the chemical hood?"

"Why are you sure he was the one that broke in last night?"

She tried to point without looking. "They're both wearing black and, judging by his height, I think he was the one that I fought in the office."

The wall next to the closet was white, much like the current state of Joe's pasty face. Next to an undergraduate degree and a postdoctorate degree, a framed certificate with an image of a trophy printed on it declared Audrey's award for best student research at Duke University. The image bothered Kendra for some reason.

She may have succeeded in keeping the Pirate from Audrey's research. She'd shipped the real drive to an address no one but her—and now Joe—knew about before buying a copy to replace it. In essence, she'd won a small victory over the Pirate, but the two individuals on the ground had lost. It wasn't a tournament Kendra had ever wanted to enter. The person responsible for creating it was out there, nameless, faceless and ready to take her and Joe's lives next. Her stomach churned, threatening to overwhelm her with nausea.

Kendra's eyes drifted down until she focused on a frayed edge of the carpet. She knew how to cope with death. She'd seen, and even been responsible for, the loss of life before. In every case, she followed tried and true steps: get out of the situation as soon as possible, stay busy, focus on the mission and eventually sleep for an entire day, then follow up with hefty servings of carbs. Comfort food was a thing for a reason. Eventually the horror would fade into the back recesses of her mind.

Without the promise of any relief in the future, it was hard to imagine ever getting a break. She'd worked so hard at burying the dark side of covert ops, that she'd never considered the benefits of a different position. If not in the field, she'd lose her sense of purpose and control, but after the past few weeks, she'd started to wonder if she ever had any in the first place. Was control all an illusion?

"Are you worried how Audrey is going to react?"

She looked up to find Joe staring at her. The thought of telling her sister made the wave of nausea wash over her again. She certainly didn't want her to be murdered and framed. She resumed the pacing once more. Movement helped her from obsessing over one detail.

"If the scientists were working for the Pirate, why would they be murdered? The bag of drugs is so obvious a plant, I'm disregarding it."

"You made sure they couldn't access any of the research. So if these two had a directive by the Pirate, they failed last night. And…it's possible they knew too much."

Her mind raced. Too many questions fought for top priority. "Tell me what you see, as an analyst."

Joe crossed his arms across his chest. "I'm starting to wonder if you think an analyst should be able to do anything you can't. I'm not a forensic scientist. I'm not a homicide detective."

"But we both know you've studied at least the basics."

He raised an eyebrow but didn't refute her claim. "I can make an educated guess at best." He pointed to the throw pillow with a hole and stuffing bits all around the floor. "They were killed by a gun with a suppressor, but the shooter used a pillow for additional help in staying quiet. They really didn't want to be heard. If I had to guess by the state of rigor mortis, their murders happened soon after our brush with them in the lab."

He looked up at the ceiling, his skin an unhealthy pasty white when it normally had a golden glow. They'd both been exposed to dead bodies before, but they'd never had to study them before. "They were whisked away the moment they left the lab while we were being herded to the demo building. They didn't have what the Pirate wanted so they were killed and, just in case there were questions about your eventual death, he added this as another frame."

"So you think they were killed here?"

His eyes met hers. "I'm afraid so. It's a frame job."

"Like a game of chess," she muttered. "Masked has made sure that one way or another we'll be forced off the board." Except these murders would frame her sister. Before she could chicken out, she stepped into the area with the bodies, bent over and reached to touch the sleeve of the woman's shirt.

Joe reached out and stopped her. "What are you doing?"

"I'm sure my DNA is all over him already, I want to make sure it's on her, as well. I don't want Audrey to be framed."

"I didn't think I'd need to remind you that you're identical twins."

It took her a second to follow his train of thought. "Haven't the police developed a new way to distinguish DNA of twins?"

His eyebrows raised. "A few years back they discovered they could melt it and look at key markers, but that's only if they *know* there is an identical twin involved. If you disappear, is the FBI going to fess up when they're trying to keep it a secret?"

Kendra wanted to scream in frustration. "I'll have to figure something out."

"There is a bright side." He pointed in the direction of the living room. "These murders, as horrible as they are, can actually help us narrow down the Pirate's identity. We just need to talk to Audrey."

She waved at the two scientists on the ground. "Unless he was never in the lab at all. Maybe Beverly's intelligence sources and analysis were wrong about him. What if he was just confident that he had enough people in place to keep Beverly out of the loop?"

Joe crossed the room, opened the coat closet door and retrieved his bag. "Whoever did this was quick and wanted to get out fast." He unzipped and zipped it. "They didn't find my ID."

"Or they did and thought it would only help the frame against us."

His face fell. "Fair enough. I'm going to check the window to make sure it's still clear. We shouldn't be here any longer than necessary."

Kendra followed him into the kitchen as he peeked through the blinds of the window. "I'll check the bedroom." She didn't make it over the threshold before she heard him groan. She spun. "What?"

"I think I've just been spotted." Shame was written all over his face. "I don't think they actually saw my face, but someone noticed the blinds move."

"Are you sure? Was it a student?" Dread weighed on her spine but she forced herself to be optimistic.

He faced her. "A student doesn't behave like that. I'm pretty sure he just sent out the news to others. We need to get out of here. Now."

She ran to the bedroom and retrieved her own backpack from underneath Audrey's bed. She'd wanted to clean the place and the bodies to make sure any fake evidence was destroyed, but she'd failed. Again. She ran out to find Joe with the coat closet door open yet again.

"I just remembered what was in here," he said. He cringed. "I know you said you're not a fan of Christmas, but considering the circumstances—" He pulled out Santa and Mrs. Claus costumes. "Fast alteration of appearance. Alternate routes. A textbook method of escape."

She hesitated. "No agent would ever put on these. It might draw extra attention."

"Which is exactly why it won't." Joe was already throwing on the gear. "Only college students would. Are you going to trust your analyst or spend time arguing?"

As if the day could get any worse. If she ever had any doubt, this sealed the deal. She definitely never had any control.

FOURTEEN

Joe grabbed the extra plate of cookies he remembered was still in the kitchen. The Santa coat and pants had slipped on right over his clothes. The pouch reserved for padding worked perfectly for his bag as well as Kendra's pack, although the discomfort of carrying the weight all at the front of his waist was hard to ignore. The beard started to itch almost instantly.

Mrs. Claus, complete with fake glasses, threw open the apartment door and moved to take off at a run.

He reached for her arm. "No, don't use the exit stairs. Go to the interior stairs. They'll be taking the perimeter ones to get up here. We need the first floor."

She nodded and they practically flew down the hallway and stairs in tandem. A quip about not needing reindeers was on the tip of the tongue, but he practiced self-control. The instinct to crack jokes—even Dad-worthy puns—after tragedy came on strong. In law enforcement, the coping strategy seemed acceptable, almost welcomed, but the move into pastoring would call for new techniques.

He hoped he'd never have to see another life taken again.

They rounded the corner as footsteps pounded above. They'd barely missed whoever was watching for them. If Joe had been working for Masked and was given the task of organizing the framing of Audrey, he'd have ordered the lookouts, likely turned agents, to hold "Audrey" there until the police arrived to confirm the frame-up story. As if on his cue, sirens reached his ears.

They stepped on the first floor. "Now where?" Kendra whispered.

"Use your lock-pick set and open the first door on your right." He'd made sure she had the set in her palm before he'd shoved her bag in his red coat.

Kendra plastered a fake smile on her face and entered the hallway, careful to avert her gaze. She moved so naturally he almost believed she loved the outfit as she turned to the door he'd mentioned. The first door to the right was also the door closest to the stairs that would have a back door facing the street.

"Merry Christmas," a voice called out. "Getting a head start, are we, Santa?"

Joe turned around to face a woman with curly hair and a Christmas sweater featuring Rudolph. She snickered at her own joke but stopped midlaugh. She carried two cloth bags filled with groceries. She leaned forward, her eyes squinting before they widened. "Audrey, is that you? I almost didn't recognize you in that getup! What are you doing?" Her wide grin turned into a concerned frown. "I thought you weren't going to do that until before the wedding, with your fiancé."

Kendra tried to hide the lock-pick set in the palm of her hand. "Um, have you met my fiancé?"

She raised an eyebrow and glanced at Joe. "This is

not your fiancé unless you have more than one or he had plastic surgery after he proposed."

"Brother, my fiancé's brother," Kendra added, smoothly, as if the woman had actually interrupted her original thought.

The woman glanced at Joe then back at Kendra as if waiting for an introduction. Joe reached out his hand. "Hi, I'm Santa, but you can call me Joe."

"Yes, I'm familiar with your work." She gestured to herself, causing the grocery bags to swing precariously close to his belly full of backpacks. "I'm Sara. Audrey and I met at staff orientation and bonded over the burned coffee and stale bagels they served." She looked down at the tray of cellophane-covered cookies and back to the door they were in front of. "You're not giving cookies to Alan, are you? I thought you couldn't stand him."

Kendra's eyebrows rose so far they almost disappeared underneath the set of white curls attached to the red hat. "Well, um, Christmas is the time to lay down our grievances, right? If I'm going to say I love this holiday, I better remember what it's really about."

The woman shook her head and opened her arms. "Only you would say that." The left grocery bag painfully bounced off Joe's knee as she moved her arms around Kendra for a hug. "Love you, girl."

Kendra fisted the hand around the lock pick and returned the hug. "Love you back." Her eyes looked wide, as if in disbelief. Two men burst through the exit doors at either end of the apartment hallways and ran toward them. Joe fought not to flinch. Both were dressed in jeans, nondescript T-shirts and hoodies—they might as well have written *undercover* on their backs.

He needed to think like Kendra, stay in character. He was just a guy dressed up in a Santa costume who was waiting for someone. Joe stepped directly behind Sara to help block Kendra's face. Sara pulled back from the hug and Kendra seamlessly spun toward the door and knocked. The three of them, looking ready to spread Christmas cheer, didn't register so much as a second glance from the men who were now running up the stairway.

Sara glanced at the door as if waiting to see what would happen.

"Maybe he's not here," Joe offered.

"Or maybe he's in the bathroom," Kendra added. "We went to all this trouble. Let's give him another minute just in case."

The woman shrugged, wandered down the hallway to the very next door and unlocked it. "If he doesn't want the cookies, you know where I live." She finally closed the door behind her.

Kendra exhaled and inserted the lock pick.

Sara's door opened once again. "Actually, I want to see his face when he answers."

Joe sidestepped diagonally to give Kendra time to pocket the pick set. "You were right in the first place. He doesn't seem to be home. Allow us to deliver the cookies to you?"

Sara grinned and held her arms wide-open, ready to accept the tray.

Joe shook his head. "Full Santa service means I need to put them on your table."

Sara laughed and shrugged. "Suit yourself, but you're not allowed to complain that I don't have a tree again." She pointed at Kendra.

"Now that does sound like something I'd do."

"I told you I'm working on it." Sara opened her door and Kendra and Joe followed as more footsteps approached. Sara closed the door behind them, shaking her head. "Wonder what they're up to."

"You can never tell on a college campus." He passed through her tidy but sparse living room and set the plate of cookies on an end table before moving to the sliding glass door.

Kendra stopped at the two cloth bags set on the counter and pulled out a box of candy canes. "How would you feel if I took these to hand out while in costume and replaced them later? I haven't had a chance to hit the store lately."

Sara pulled her chin back in surprise. "I guess it's okay. I mean they're really good in hot cocoa."

Kendra popped open the box and handed her one wrapped candy cane with a smile. "So are the cookies."

Joe unlocked the back door and slid it open. "Speaking of antics on campus, I think I want to train for the big night and sneak out the back."

Sara raised an eyebrow as Kendra offered an awkward laugh and crossed the room, candy canes in hand, to join him. "What can I say? He's a bit weird."

"Good. You'll fit right into his family." Sara giggled at her joke and waved before she lifted the cellophane off the plate of cookies.

Kendra closed the glass door behind her and the stood on the small cement patio. "I thought handing out candy canes might help us sell the costume until we get off campus."

"Perfect, but it might not have been necessary." He

led her through a grouping of sweetshade trees. They crossed the street, off campus, but students walked and biked nearby. Kendra passed out candy canes until she had only two left. By that time, they approached an assisted-living facility he'd noticed earlier.

"While I've never found Santa to be particularly attractive, it's nice to know you'll age well."

"Why, Mrs. Claus, are you saying I look good with a beard?"

"You always look good." She rolled her eyes but her cheeks flushed. "Are you sure your purpose isn't to go into covert ops yourself? You handled that well—unorthodoxly, but still well."

"No, I have no desire for anything covert." He glanced over his shoulder as he led her into a small enclave in between two of the assisted-living buildings. He removed the beard and allowed himself five seconds to scratch his chin. Kendra had already taken his cue and removed the outer Mrs. Claus hat and curls.

"Where should we put them?"

"How about on that table. Maybe the staff will see it as a gift and entertain the residents."

Kendra groaned. "I'm going to have to buy new costumes for Audrey."

"That's positive thinking. Someday everything is going to get back to normal." He set the pile on an outdoor table and led her back to the street. The adrenaline was beginning to fade again. He desperately needed sleep, but according to the brochures he'd studied while in the security waiting room, there were motels nearby for visitors. Just two more streets over there was a motel that was cheapest on the list. As long as nothing was living in or under the mattresses, waiting to bite him when he closed his eyes, he'd sleep. His eyes drooped at the thought.

Kendra took her bag back from him and swung it over her shoulder. "I almost forgot to turn my phone back on." She clicked the power button. Ten seconds later the phone vibrated violently.

"I've missed ten messages from Audrey." Kendra opened her mouth in horror. "We're only supposed to contact each other in emergencies."

Over a mile off campus, they reached the historic Route 66. Kendra did her best to keep up with Joe's fast strides while trying to read through Audrey's text messages.

"It'd be better if we were somewhere secure before we address those. We need to be alert," he said.

Her heart pounded wildly. How long had Audrey been trying to reach them? Worst-case scenarios and visions of her twin injured—or worse—flashed through her mind. "But it's my sister and everything that could go wrong, has gone wrong. So you stay alert while I read."

He reached for her arm and pulled her sideways, closer to him. "I'd like to be alert for danger in the form of people, not mailboxes."

She looked up to see he had kept her from running right into a commercial mailbox, but she ignored his plea because she'd already opened the messages application. The first message read:

Are you okay? Very odd communication. Need advice. Think we need to talk.

Her heart rate slowed a little. Maybe Kendra hadn't failed to keep her sister safe.

The message repeated for a second time but with the addition of 100%, their agreed-upon code that would prove it was Audrey who was messaging.

The third message read:

This is getting serious. I know we said no voice mails but you're not answering your phone. We need to talk.

The fourth message repeated the third with the same addition of 100%.

She groaned. "Okay, maybe it's not so bad. I think she kept forgetting the code."

Except the pattern of escalating messages made it clear the matter was indeed urgent. The tenth and final message read:

SOS. You have two hours to call me back or I'm taking matters into my own hands. 100%

"She says it's an emergency." She glanced at the time sent. "I have ten minutes to answer this before Audrey does something potentially dangerous."

"We're here," he said, pointing at a run-down sign with only half the letters still visible. "See if she can wait five minutes. I just want us to be in a secure room before you talk." His eyes met hers. "Tell her the analyst insists."

Kendra's brain fought to remember her agreed-upon code for half a second before she texted a reply.

Stand down. Am safe. Promise to call from secure location in a few minutes. 2*

It's about time!

It's about time! 100%

"She responded," Kendra told Joe. Sandwiched in
between the buildings, a small motel stood. It seemed
hard to believe they were less than a mile from Caltech.
It was as if they'd left a suburb and entered an old city.

He pointed to a sitting area hidden behind a tall pillar. She stood as nonchalantly as possible behind it while
he checked them in. Within two minutes, Joe joined her
and led her to two doors that still used old-fashioned
metal keys. "Thankfully they accepted the Visa Gift
cards and were able to give us adjoining rooms."

Inside, they found a modest set of rooms with blue
walls and white bedding. He sank down on the edge of
the one he first saw. "Okay. You better call her now. I'm
not sure how much good I'll be to anyone in a minute."

Kendra didn't need to be told twice. She dialed and
waited for it to ring.

"I've been worried sick!" Audrey's voice came on
the line. "You better have some solid reasoning why
you've been ignoring my calls."

Joe's left eyebrow raised. "Put it on speaker."

Kendra tapped the button but didn't get a chance to
warn Audrey because she couldn't get a word in edge-
wise.

"I got this email last night from Wyatt, and I didn't
know what to think. I spent most of the night panicked

and pacing until my mom made a steamer—it's milk that she puts the tiniest bit of delicious syrup in. You have to try it sometime."

"Audrey—" Her sister's mind ran a mile a minute and could sometimes jump to tangents.

"You told me not to check any email, and I haven't answered any emails, but I did check my personal email account. Not my work account. I know even that is against the rules you gave me, but you don't know what it's like waiting without any—"

"Actually, I do know what that's like to wait like that," Kendra finally interjected. "And from a hospital room of all places." One look at Joe's weary face told her not to take any time on personal matters, and there also wasn't room to express her frustration that Audrey hadn't followed her instructions about avoiding email altogether. "What did the email say?"

"Oh. He said he had come to Caltech earlier than planned—we already knew that, obviously—but he says that when he stopped by my laboratory he was met by my doppelgänger, a look-alike imposter that could never be me, unless I'd taken a leave of my senses and resorted to illicit drug use." Audrey pulled in a sharp breath. "What did you do? Why would he think I'd gone crazy?"

So far there was nothing Audrey had relayed that warranted an SOS alert. "I didn't know about your circuit-board-themed tree. He had brought you an ornament."

"He did?" Her voice softened. "Oh. Well, I told you it's harder to switch places than you'd think."

Joe tilted back his head and closed his eyes.

"Was that all?" Kendra urged.

"He said you'd been shot. Were you?"

Joe's eyes flew open and he leaned forward. "Audrey, what specifically did he write?"

"Oh. Hi, Joe. Might've been nice if my sister had let me know I was on speakerphone. Glad to hear you're alive, too. He wrote… Let me pull it up." The sound of tapping fingernails and a couple clicks on a keyboard could be heard. "Okay. 'Not only do you have a look-alike trying, no doubt, to steal your research while you're away, but she was in a gunfight last night and taken to the hospital. In the event you have a sister you've never mentioned, I thought you should know right away. And if you don't, I think you should be concerned about the safety of your research.'"

"It's a trap." Kendra sank down in the armchair in the corner and rested the phone on her knee.

Joe shook his head. "We can't jump to conclusions."

Something in the back of her mind demanded attention. She sat upright. "What did you say about his favorite movie?"

"*The Princess Bride*, but everyone—"

"Who was his favorite character?" Kendra nodded at Joe with a meaningful gaze, willing him to see where she was going with the series of questions.

"Westley, but I don't see why that—"

"Also known as the Dread Pirate Roberts," Joe interrupted. "And also not proof, Kendra. I'll grant you, it is another pirate with a near-mythical reputation."

Kendra held up her index finger. "You can't deny that I didn't get into a gunfight or go to the hospital last night. Where would he get that?"

"It's possible Wyatt wrote that because he really

thought you were dead and out of the picture." He rubbed his forehead. "I really am tired. You're right. Whatever the reason, it's still a ploy to get Audrey here. But we don't know if it's to get her back as his girlfriend or for more nefarious reasons, like stealing research. It looks bad, but we can never assume."

Audrey was silent for a brief moment. "You're not implying Wyatt is..." She blew out a forceful breath that produced feedback on Kendra's phone speaker. "Is everyone in my life something they're not?"

"Apparently that's our family legacy," Kendra said, the bitter words slipping out before she thought about it.

"What's that supposed to mean?"

Kendra couldn't tell her now, over the phone, about Beverly and their double-agent father. That wouldn't be fair, yet she was dying to tell her. "Someone told me recently that you can never really know everything about a person." Her eyes met Joe's.

He responded with a hard frown, then stood and paced.

"Did you find out something? Are you trying to say I shouldn't trust Lee?" Audrey asked. "Do you know something I don't know?"

"No, she's not saying that at all," Joe answered. He looked up. "I'm sure she was referring to Wyatt. Right?"

If Kendra could rewind time and start the conversation over, she would in a heartbeat. Her stomach turned to concrete. "Of course I mean Wyatt. I'm also grumpy at our lack of progress and lashing out."

No matter what complicated feelings Kendra was trying to sort out for herself about Beverly and their biological father, she had no right to mess up her sister's happily-ever-after. And, judging by the wording of Wyatt's email, he assumed Audrey had no idea what was going on the past couple of days, which kept her safe. He also knew her as a genius and had a fondness for her. Kendra wasn't about to jeopardize that.

"Oh." Audrey's voice dropped. "It is a stressful situation. What do you think I should do with this email?"

Joe spun on his heel. "If he wants to set a trap, we set a trap first. Then we'll know who we're really dealing with. Kendra, pick a location that has a flight coming in late tonight. Audrey, I want you to reply via email. Tell him, in your own words, that he was freaking you out with talks of a look-alike. Let him know that you just received word about your laboratory blowing up—"

"My what?" Audrey's voice raised an octave. "Please tell me you're kidding."

Joe's stricken face almost made Kendra laugh.

"It was a minor diversion to get everyone out of the lab." Kendra bit her lip. This also wasn't the time to reveal that two people had been murdered in her apartment.

Joe nodded. "Yes, we'll explain all of that later. Anyway, let him know you're ending your trip early, include whatever flight Kendra chooses for you—so he won't really know your current location—and ask Wyatt if he would mind picking you up from the airport. Except it'll be Kendra waiting for him, not you." Joe sat down on the bed, leaned back and closed his eyes. "Now if you'll excuse me I just need a few minutes of sleep before we go on the offensive and end this or die trying."

FIFTEEN

Joe woke with a start. He rushed to the adjoining door between their rooms and knocked.

"Good morning." Kendra opened the door wide. Everything had been removed from her backpack and she appeared to be sorting it in heaps, including a pile of cash.

"Morning? I slept that long?"

"No, I meant it figuratively. It's five o'clock in the afternoon." She had changed, and judging by her damp, wavy hair, she'd cleaned up. "How do you feel? If you didn't wake up in the next twenty minutes, I would've insisted. You have enough time to shower and get dressed before we go over the plan. I need an analyst's take on it before I can call it good."

Joe didn't need to be told twice. He grabbed his bag, showered and then returned to her room fully awake and, more important, clean and ready to go. A knock sounded at her front door.

Kendra pulled out her gun and moved to the open closet area. "I ordered us food." She handed Joe cash. "If you wouldn't mind."

Kendra remained hidden, gun at the ready, as he opened the door. The pizza guy shoved the box and a large bottle of Dr Pepper into Joe's hands. In exchange, Joe handed him the cash. "Keep the change."

The smell of food made him weak with hunger. He couldn't remember the last time they'd eaten. Kendra put away her gun and grabbed the box from his hands. "I hope you like soda. I'm desperate for caffeine, but there's no coffee maker in these rooms."

"You have to pay extra for that," Joe commented. Something so small served as a reminder that if they didn't take down this Masked organization soon, he could say goodbye to all the nice amenities in his life.

She placed the box down on an empty spot on the tall dresser and flipped open the lid. Normally, he hated olives but he didn't take the time to pick anything off the supreme pizza before shoving the piece in his mouth. They ate standing up, since there was only one chair in the corner without a table.

"I thought we needed sustenance in case it's our last meal." Kendra spoke in between bites. Her eyebrows rose. "Besides inhaling food—" Joe was already on his second piece "—what's the first thing you're going to do when we're free to choose?"

He picked up a third piece. "I like your optimism." The sentiment seemed premature, though, as they hadn't gone over the plan yet.

"Don't get used to it. It's not normal. I think I've been around you too long." She grinned and finally started on her second piece.

Joe picked up his fourth piece and forced himself to slow down. "After this experience, I think I'm going to focus more on relationships than my career. Not that I won't always try my best, but I think I'd like to trust Him more to guide my direction."

She studied him for a moment and nodded. "Think you'll settle down? Married? Two kids?" She filled two plastic cups with soda.

He accepted the drink from her. "That is still the American dream, right?"

She shrugged. "How would I know? I've been living among thieves for the past few years." She took a gulp then set the cup on the dresser. "But I could see the dream come true for you. You would make someone a good husband." She shook her head. "Whereas I could never marry a pastor."

He forced a laugh at the new information. "Okay. Thanks for the heads-up, I guess?" He tried to play it off as humorous but something about her statement wounded him for no logical reason. As if it would be so horrible for a woman to marry him simply because of his occupation? But that wasn't what she said. She said *she* could never marry a pastor. It didn't bother him any less.

She flushed. "Sorry, that came out of left field. I'm not implying that you asked or ever…you know, intended. I mean, in general, I don't think I could handle life as a pastor's wife."

He struggled to know what to answer in reply. Maybe it would be best to joke that he would return the diamond promptly and cancel the proposal. He couldn't bring himself to make light of her declaration, though. "Okay. I'll bite. Why?"

"Joe…" She kept her eyes averted and twisted her

hands, something she never did. "I've taken down criminals." She glanced up. "With force."

"If you're trying to say you've had to kill someone before, I know, Kendra."

"I took down a shooter at Stanford before his brother shot me back, and it wasn't the first time I had to use force." She held her hands out as if in surrender. "Pastors' wives are expected to be gentle—"

"If you're referring to a certain passage about women, 'gentle and quiet *spirit*' is what the verse says. It doesn't mean—"

"Okay, fine, but even if I put that aside. Pastors' wives are supposed to be able to make conversation with the other women in the church. Imagine me at the annual ladies tea or luncheon." She turned sideways as if talking to an imaginary person. "Oh, you want me to pray about Billy being bullied at school? Tell me more. Details." She turned to Joe with wide eyes. "See? I wouldn't be able to just stand by. I'd get names and take care of it. And that's just a mild example."

Joe fought not to laugh. "That might not be a bad thing. I'm sure you'd handle the matter tactfully."

She held up her hand and leaned forward. "That's not the point and you know it."

"So, what about a pastor? Does the standard remain the same?" He set down his own cup. His gut heated even thinking about it. "Do you think a soldier who has killed in the line of duty should never become one?"

Her eyes widened. "No, that's not—"

"Or what about someone who previously worked in law enforcement? Should they be disqualified?"

She stepped closer and put her hand over his. "Joe,

that's not what I was trying to say. This week…you saved my life when you shot—"

He frowned, fighting the sudden tension in his neck and back. "I would do it again if it meant saving your life, Kendra." He cleared his throat. This was about her, not him. "But if it's okay for a pastor with a past to serve, why wouldn't it be okay for you to marry one? Or," he hastily added, "serve in a church or attend a ladies tea."

"I guess I have a mental image of what a pastor's wife should be, and I'm nothing like it. I mean I could never be like a normal wife…or a normal mother." Her face dropped. "I'm sure if I was more like Audrey, then maybe…"

As if layers were being removed one at a time, Joe was starting to suspect the unexpected discussion wasn't about being a pastor's wife at all. Whatever was bothering her went deeper. The thought relieved him ever so slightly—not that he was actually thinking about her as his… Well, now he was, and it didn't seem like a horrible thing at all. But, he needed to focus on her, without any underlying feelings attached.

"I hate to break it to you, Kendra, but there is no such thing as normal. Your parents, your siblings, love you for you. That's not going to change when they meet Audrey. There might be comparisons, but there'll only be joy from them, celebrating the differences of what makes you unique."

Her eyes shone. He'd hit the real issue right on the head. She blinked rapidly, as she looked up at the ceiling, clearly trying to rein in emotions. "I know. I'm being stupid."

He placed his arm around her shoulder and patted

her arm. Her spine stiffened and he let go, as he assumed she didn't want to be comforted, but she turned into him. He quickly adjusted and wrapped his arms around her for a hug. She didn't hesitate and laid her cheek against his beating heart. Her arms wrapped around his waist.

"I have no doubt in my mind that when you fall in love—" his voice grew husky and he decided he'd said enough, but his mouth kept running "—that blessed guy is going to love you for you. You will be their ideal of a wife, and maybe someday a mom." *Even if that guy isn't me.* The thought hit him from left field.

She pulled back just enough to look up at him. Her eyes dilated but the green with brown edges still captivated him. She glanced quickly at his lips and back at his eyes again. "Thank you."

Kendra was in his arms. She didn't even understand how she'd gotten there; the hug felt natural a minute ago, but somehow it meant more now. Her stomach heated as she fought back nervousness. The truth was she wanted to kiss him. Her gaze drifted back to his lips.

He tilted his head and leaned down to—

Her muscles tensed. "What are you doing?" She took a giant step out of his arms.

He blinked. "I, uh…"

The level of awkwardness was off the charts, and Kendra wasn't sure how to switch gears. She could've handled the moment more tactfully, but she'd panicked.

Joe cleared his throat. "I think I need more caffeine." He refilled his cup and moved like a tortoise, sipping the soda in unusually small amounts. Maybe she should apologize if she'd led him to believe she wanted him to kiss her.

For a split second, though, she *had* wanted to lean in. They were both exhausted and stressed, that was all. Things like that happened. Though, it had never happened once in all the stressful situations she'd been in with her partner, Lee. So that excuse wasn't worth mentioning.

Well, it didn't matter. The moment was gone and they needed to get past it. "You know, we should probably focus on the plan. We're starting to get down to the wire."

He nodded but avoided eye contact. "Your hair looks more like Audrey's when it's wavy like that, but what about her clothes? I've only seen her in Christmas attire."

"True. But I'm hoping the color will pass." She fingered the edge of the long red pullover. The black soft pants resembled dress pants in form, but the fabric appeared to be more of an activewear texture. "My sister and I might choose completely different clothes for work and dates, but we do have the same taste in loungewear. I feel pretty confident she'd want to dress comfortably for air travel." She picked up her phone and opened the browser to the airport schematics. "Um, so back to the plan."

Joe leaned over to look and their shoulders touched. "There will be security cameras everywhere, so that helps the safety factor. He's not going to pull a gun on you at the airport. Masked can't have bought out the entire TSA."

"So I had Audrey email a rough pickup time to Wyatt without any airline or flight number. She asked him to meet her at this pickup, near the baggage claim." She pointed at the section of the airport map. "I find him, ask some questions as he leads me back to his car. If we reach his car before I get an inkling of whether he's after Audrey as a girlfriend or for research, I'll stall and say I forgot luggage or something. If I get any indication it's all about the research, that's good enough confirmation for me that he's the Pirate or working in close proximity. I go back in the airport, meet you at the counter and we fly back to that hospital and use the same drop spot you used for Beverly. Hopefully the NCS director gets the information. I don't know who else to trust without a way to contact her."

"There's a lot of problems with this plan. What if he forces you into the car?"

She handed him the phone so he could study the airport without standing so close. "You know what LAX airport pickup is like. There will be cars everywhere."

"But if you get near and he's pointing a gun at you, then what?"

"You follow me."

"I can't park a rental car at an airport pickup. I'll be told to move on within sixty seconds. The honking would be deafening."

"So you take a cab. Not ideal, but I'm sure you can manage the worst-case scenario. I don't think he's going to risk pulling a gun on me at the airport parking lot."

He shook his head. "What if he does want the research, but it turns out he's only another hired hand, like those scientists?"

Kendra threw up her hands. "This was your suggested plan!"

"Right before I passed out from exhaustion." He

paced. "We can still make this viable. The only way this works is if he arrives and you ask him to come into the airport to wait with you for your luggage."

Her eyes lit up. "Brilliant. That way I don't need to buy any luggage beforehand."

"Once inside the airport, I show up and sit down with him and have a nice little chat until we conclude whether he's the Pirate or not."

"But Beverly said not to take him down, only to ID him. How do we make an arrest without knowing whom to trust? And then there's the little problem of evidence."

"Beverly has loads of that."

Kendra nodded. "Which we don't have access to. If we tip him off that we *know* he's the one, even if we manage to get out of town, he'll most definitely have Masked looking and ready to take us down."

"That's it." Joe's eyes lit up. "We admit fully who we are and why."

"Have you completely lost it? You didn't get enough sleep."

"No, think about it. How did Masked get started and grow? A federal employee, or in this case a contractor, managed to recruit other employees to sell information, starting small, to the highest bidder. We want in."

Kendra froze, replaying his words. "We want in," she said slowly. "We *do* have the research. I'm absolutely not Audrey, and this was all a plan to make a big payday."

"We're both rogue FBI agents on leave. We've been trying to track down how to get in on the Masked payroll for years but didn't have anything valuable to give until now."

Kendra nodded—the ideas for her new cover were

coming rapidly now. "And if he already knows our identities, you claim that you were trying to get close enough to Beverly to find out what the next target was for Masked so you could get in on it."

"And you arrived to join me because we're partners."

"After I'd had a little plastic surgery work done. I already looked like Audrey but I made it look convincing. I took over her email and she had no idea what was going on. It's important we make that clear to him. We want money in exchange for the research." She nodded. "So we've got our plan and a backup plan."

"The escape plan is to stay in the airport, fly back to the hospital drop zone, give the info we gathered and go off the grid."

"This is good. I feel good about this." Her heart wouldn't slow down, though, perhaps from the surge of adrenaline. Without Joe thinking through all the possibilities, she would've ruined their chances. It was as if a well-lit billboard had been placed in front of her that read Your Pride Has Definitely Been Holding You Back. Maybe she'd have had more results in the past if she'd treated Lee more like a partner than a fellow employee. For some reason, it was easier with Joe. She didn't feel like she always needed to take the lead with him.

Joe threw his bag over his shoulder. "Now, all that's left is prayer that all goes according to plan."

"Or that if He has a better plan, He makes it known to us."

He hesitated at the door. "Couldn't have said it better myself."

SIXTEEN

Waking up just before the sun went down messed with Joe's sense of time. They picked up a shuttle and were on their way to the airport within the hour. For the most part, they remained silent during the trip. Though they sat in the back seat, the couple in the middle row kept the driver busy with conversation.

Traffic seemed lighter than usual. They passed by an exit sign for Caltech. "If we do end up needing a permanent change of plans," Joe began, careful of his wording in the presence of others, "I would hope to spend it on a university or college campus somewhere."

Kendra's soft smile changed her entire face, as if it lit up from the inside. "That sounds like you. Spend the rest of your time collecting every degree imaginable." She frowned. "What surprises me is why you didn't choose campus ministry from the start."

"What?"

"You know, college ministry. Some national organizations and churches invest in that. It's for undergraduates primarily."

He blinked. He'd never been to a campus ministry

before. "That wasn't an available emphasis in my seminary. My bachelor's was also online so I can't say I have personal experience in that area."

She faced forward. "Well, I did. It was a national organization, but a lot of the local churches supported it. It's probably where my family's faith finally became personal. The meetings weren't set up like a formal church, though. There was lots of Bible study, but it was more interactive than any church service. We spent a lot of time discussing our beliefs and what they meant for our lives." She smiled. "It's the only time I could fathom what the type of community described in Acts could look like in real life. It's too bad you didn't have that, I think you would've liked it."

The statement awakened something inside of him, but he didn't know what it meant or what to do with it. Maybe it was just regret that he'd missed out on the full undergraduate experience. The people in the middle row turned around and asked Kendra why they had come to the area.

Kendra answered easily about visiting the J. Paul Getty Museum. The driver dropped them off at Arrivals. Kendra stepped out at Southwest. They'd gone over the map and knew that from here on out, eyes could be watching. Joe remained in the shuttle with darkened windows until the driver stopped at Delta.

Once inside the airport, he kept his eyes down and made his way to the elevators. Kendra would be, by now, halfway down the escalators to the baggage claim and Arrivals.

A few minutes later, he stationed himself behind a cement pillar, one where the security camera would be at his back while he kept an eye on the automatic glass doors where Kendra planned to exit. He acted as if he was reading his phone and waiting, even though he was staring at his blank messages screen. The two-way radios they'd used on campus had been left behind in their rush to escape the demolished building. What a waste.

His spot enabled him to watch for Wyatt as the cars rushed by, with only quick stops for other passengers. Aside from the backpack on his shoulder, the only weight was his gun, loaded and ready, and his FBI badge in case guns needed to be drawn, after all.

There. He spotted her. Kendra had pulled her hair into a ponytail and was wearing a pleasant smile. If he hadn't noticed her stiffened posture and the way her eyes roved for signs of weapons, he'd guess she was Audrey, especially from afar. So far, he hadn't seen a driver or anyone approaching that resembled Wyatt.

He peeked around the column and felt a sharp metal barrel in his side. "No sudden movements." The male voice spoke firmly. "DEA." Joe took the man to be true to his word, but slowly looked over his shoulder. The man was dressed in a blue jacket with the Drug Enforcement Administration embroidered logo on the front. A second man appeared at his other side. The first man tapped Joe's hip and held up a bag of white powder. "Oh, look at what I found. Cocaine, probably with the intent to distribute."

Joe debated his options. He might be able to pull a stunt that could enable him to get enough room to pull his own gun and badge. But that could backfire without a follow-up plan. He looked toward the exit to see if Kendra could see what was going on, but instead only saw the back of three jackets, all labeled with the yellow DEA. They had her surrounded.

The remaining passengers walking past had varying reactions. Some seemed curious but wanted to keep their distance. He didn't see anyone pull out their iPhone, though even if they had, the agents were doing a great job in covering three sides of Kendra.

A white SUV with a blue stripe and the Homeland Security logo pulled up to the curb with silent blinking emergency lights. "Which is it? Are you from DEA or DHS?"

"Time to take a ride," the man on the left said.

"What, no Miranda warning?" Without a plan of action, Joe couldn't risk putting Kendra in jeopardy. The best idea he had was to stall and buy some time to figure out a new tactic.

"Pretty sure you know you won't be needing any rights." They roughly removed his backpack and gun. "Concealed weapon. No carry permit," the man practically yelled before shoving him into the back seat.

A second later Kendra joined him, her face flushed.

He reached for her hands, searching for signs of abuse. "Did they hurt you?"

She shook her head ever so slightly. "No, but I think the Pirate just declared checkmate."

The sirens kicked on, and through the metal grid separating them from the driver and passenger, two men dressed as officers didn't so much as give them a second glance. The passenger grabbed a cell phone. "We've got her and the guy." He turned to look over his shoulder at Kendra. "What was your favorite burrito place for middle-of-the-night runs while you were at Duke?"

She blinked for a second. What a ridiculous question, and she was sure the answer would not be the nationally known chain, Qdoba, her personal favorite because of the queso. Besides, they weren't open in the middle of the night. And, knowing her sister, she would never pick a chain restaurant. So what would Audrey do in this situation?

"Tell Wyatt," she finally answered, "that if he wants the answer to that question, he needs to ask me himself. When I'm not in the back of the police car on the bogus charge of intent to distribute cocaine." She increased the volume with each word as she leaned forward. "Are you trying to ruin my reputation, Wyatt? What's going on?"

"Sit back," the officer hollered. He held up the phone to his ear. Kendra might've been mistaken but she thought she'd heard a laugh on the other end. "Yes, sir. Understood."

He hung up and motioned with his chin. "He wants to talk to her at the place."

Kendra exhaled. She couldn't play the indignant card forever, but she didn't want to know what was planned if she'd simply answered wrong. The sky had darkened quickly to a midnight blue and the stars twinkled brightly. They pulled into an underground parking garage. An automatic gate closed behind the SUV. So much for an attempted escape once they got out of the vehicle. Sounds of drums and cheering sounded in the distance.

"Stupid holiday parade," the driver muttered.

"Works in our favor," the passenger muttered. He opened the door and glanced at Kendra. "Screams won't do you any good. Play nice and you'll get to speak to Mr. Nardelli."

For the moment, she decided to play along. She glanced at Joe and gave him a nod. The man yanked her by the arm and roughly pulled her arms behind her back and clipped on handcuffs. "Really? You tell Wyatt he better have an amazing Christmas present for me to make up for this treatment."

The man spun her around but didn't respond. Instead he gave her a little shove. "Move it."

They rode the elevator to the tenth floor. Kendra second-guessed her decision to cooperate as the numbers climbed. If they did escape, each floor meant increased chances of getting caught. The men led them to a room with no furniture, a cement floor and plain white walls. There was one window in the room, but it had bars on the outside of it. "Who needs bars ten flights up?" she muttered.

The men left and slammed the door behind them.

Joe walked toward it. "All the windows in this building, as well as the couple we drove by, were covered in bars. I'm guessing this didn't use to be the safest place to work. Maybe they're revitalizing the area. Though, this building seems abandoned." He stared up at the lone light bulb. "The room doesn't seem prepared for us. I don't see signs of a bug or camera, which isn't necessarily a good thing. We might want someone watching if we need something."

He continued to look around, calm and serene, as if he was waiting in line to be let into a movie theater.

"We need to stay alert and figure out—"

"Stick to the plan," Joe said.

"Excuse me? We are so far off the initial idea, we would need a day by boat to simply get in viewing distance of the plan."

"No, listen, we still have leverage if we—"

The sound of the doorknob twisting ended their argument early. Kendra whirled around to find Wyatt, looking smug in the doorway. "Sorry about the handcuffs. It's been a rough couple of days. Precautionary."

"If you wanted to win me back, Wyatt, handcuffs were the wrong tactic. Although, I have to admit you must've become a smooth talker. How did you get so many agents to do your bidding?"

He smiled. "Oh, the DEA? It only took one real officer, but you don't know which one now, do you? The fact is you don't need to turn that many, very few really. And you might suspect the high-level soldiers or officers, but rarely do you need to go after them. The lowest level with access to the information you seek is the safest and most lucrative way to go. For many, it's a onetime thing and I never contact them again. They get paid, I get paid and countries get more equal footing. Everyone wins."

He was talking too much, telling her more than she imagined. That didn't bode well for a chance at survival. Maybe he didn't intend to ever let them go. "Everyone wins?" She doubted a debate with her would change his mind, though. "I don't exactly feel like a winner standing here in handcuffs."

He walked forward and looked into her eyes. She stared right back, noticing the wrinkles and the sunspots on Wyatt's face. He was either *much* older than Audrey was led to believe, or he wasn't handling the stress of a life of treason as well as he pretended.

"What was our first date?" he asked.

"My fiancé is next to me. We've both been kidnapped. I'm not going to play a round of twenty questions."

"Then stop pretending you're Audrey."

"You're right. She's not. She's also not the one calling the shots," Joe said. "We arranged for the real Professor Clark to take a trip so we could come to Caltech on business. We've wanted in on Masked as soon as we got wind of it. We tried to make contact with you through another professor we believed was working for you, until someone tried to take us out."

Wyatt glanced at Kendra. "You were trying to talk to Beverly."

She nodded. "Until you blew her up."

This was the moment of truth. He'd either admit it or deny it and Kendra would finally know if she was still alive.

He turned to Joe instead, though. "What did you think you'd gain by coming here?"

"We were certain it would only be a matter of time until you would go after Audrey Clark's research." His chin jutted toward Kendra. "She looked similar enough it didn't take much work to make her look like the real thing. We planned to offer our services to your organization, but when Beverly disappeared, we decided to take matters into our own hands. Bottom line—you pay us, and then you get the research. Simple. We want a win-win scenario."

Wyatt studied Kendra as if in a new light. "And what about Audrey?"

"She won a vacation. She's safe and has no idea someone has taken over her lab, her email, her apartment… Although I imagine she'll figure it out real quick when she returns to find her lab blown up and two murdered scientists on her floor."

Wyatt frowned. He turned back to Joe. "And you are?"

"Joe Rose, FBI."

Kendra hated that he was using his real name.

"And her?"

"An excellent actress whose name stays with me. She'll be changing her identity again soon enough so you don't need to worry."

Wyatt looked both of them up and down before he left the room without a word.

She spun around. "Why'd you tell them your name?"

"They already had my badge."

She closed her eyes. This was getting worse by the minute. "Do you think he's going to be willing to make a deal? What's your take on him?"

"Not what I hoped. That was not a man that looked open to negotiation." Joe averted his eyes, shifting them upward as if simultaneously answering her and praying. "We need a new plan. Now."

SEVENTEEN

Joe didn't want to say the other thing on his mind, but he felt the need. "We need to prepare ourselves that we might not get to leave." They had achieved what they set out to do. They had identified the Pirate, but Wyatt knew it, as well. What were the chances that he would let them go?

She stepped forward, closer to him. "Every time I prepare for a mission—" her shoulders wiggled as her frown deepened "—I have to be okay with the possibility that I might not come back alive, and I need to be at peace with that." She smiled. "But I also have a firm belief that I'm not going down without using every bit of strength I have to stay alive." Her chin lifted and her neck strained, as if she was fighting against the handcuffs.

"No offense, but I think physics is more on my side to break out of handcuffs by force, and I can tell you it's not going to happen. You might as well stop hurting yourself trying."

Her entire face scrunched up as if she was still wrestling against the metal until there was a small click. She beamed and brought her arms around to her front. A small piece of black plastic hung from the keyhole. She bent over and took off her left shoe. "My grandpa, on my dad's side, was a retired US Navy SEAL, and before he passed away, he told me and my brothers that we should always have certain tools on our person." She lifted the sole and pulled out another plastic key, then gestured for him to turn around. "Sometimes I use three large bandages and use two of them like a pouch to stick on my waist, but I usually try to choose pants that have a small pocket on the back waist. They're usually intended for a smartphone but all I need is to hide one of these keys in the zipper handle. Never gets found in a pat-down."

Her arms brushed against his as she attempted to unlock his handcuffs. "Only problem is they're cheap and bend. One use only. Good for us I always carry two in case they decide to handcuff me in front." Another click sounded and the metal released around Joe's wrists.

"You're amazing." He studied the door. "They're likely to have that guarded. I do think we need to get out of here right away."

She strode to the window. "The windows have bars. That leaves one option." She pointed to the door. "When someone opens it, we try to use the element of surprise. They don't know we aren't handcuffed."

One of the indentions on the door trim caught his eye. It didn't match the others. He approached the trim to study the odd-looking screw. Unfortunately, it wasn't a screw at all. "I'm afraid they do know." He pointed to the miniature wireless camera. His stomach churned, suddenly unhappy with what might have been his last meal, after all.

Kendra's shoulders fell. "It's my fault. I should've checked the room myself."

Her words made him feel worse, as if a punch to the gut. He thought he'd been thorough. He'd failed her.

She leaned up against the wall. A sheen appeared on her eyes and she closed them. "We're out of options." The sounds of a marching band swelled in the distance. "Might be more appropriate if they played that drumroll famously used before an execution instead of 'A Holly Jolly Christmas.'" She offered a soft, sad smile. "You probably like Christmas parades, huh? What exactly do you like about the holiday?"

He recognized the sudden need to talk about Christmas as a plea to get her mind off what was about to happen. His throat burned with frustration that he didn't have any other ideas of his own. If he thought punching a hole in the wall would get them anywhere, he would do it in a heartbeat.

Instead, Joe moved to stand next to her and leaned against the same wall. He might not be a super agent, but he could at least do this for her. Make sure her last few moments felt like time with a friend. "I don't know about parades, per se, but I guess I like gifts."

"Figures." She laughed.

He smiled. "No, I don't mean the getting. The giving is supposed to remind us that He gave us the greatest gift of all. We didn't and never will deserve the goodness of a Savior, but we still were given one. It was the ultimate rescue mission."

She turned to him, eyes wide. "A rescue mission. I

never thought of it that way, but I guess it was. I can get behind that." She groaned. "It's silly, given what we're about to face, but I regret not getting—"

She glanced at the camera and back at him, and Joe didn't know whether it had an audio feed or not.

"—I regret not getting a present for the big day," she said. Her tone made it clear she meant Audrey but didn't want to use her name. As far as Masked was concerned, they still didn't know Audrey and Kendra were sisters, and they wanted to keep it that way. "Sometimes, I think there's nothing I'd want more than to live the life that awaits her—the one of a wife and a mother. Except, I'm not sure I'd even care what I did to make a living as long as it supported those two things—" She blushed but forged ahead. "But then I wonder if every decision I've made so far is a result of the path my biological mom started for me, by where I was placed and her anonymous tips helping me along the way. But my adoptive mom always wanted the life of a wife and mother, so maybe that desire is all a part of my upbringing. I go around in circles. So, who am I really? It'd kind of be nice to know before I die, wouldn't it?"

"Most people would agree I had about as normal a childhood as anyone could want. I was safe, I was loved, I was nurtured. Yet, I'm still a thirty-year-old man who doesn't know what he wants to be when he grows up."

She offered a sheepish smile. "You're saying it's normal to doubt the desires of my heart?"

He shook his head. "I'd never downplay anything you're feeling. I'm sure the circumstances of your childhood impact you, but your struggles are relatable. They aren't who you are, though. I'm paraphrasing, but there's a verse in Proverbs that says if we trust and acknowledge Him in all areas of our life that He will direct our paths."

"I'm certainly hoping He'll step in and do that now."

Joe sighed. "The path might not always be what we want, but I've felt a new freedom this week that I haven't in years. Ironic since we've been running for our lives." He turned and looked into her eyes, and for a second he could imagine they weren't about to be killed, as long as they focused on each other. "You are a God-fearing, strong woman who wants to make a difference in the world. You're action-oriented. You have an insane work ethic, choosing to help others, sometimes to the detriment of your own—"

"You do realize all those things can be said about you, too, right? Well, except for the woman part." There was laughter in her voice. "I guess we're more alike than I realized. We just approach it differently."

"Then I guess I needed to hear those words, too. What I was trying to get at is our identity goes much deeper than our day-to-day roles."

"I can tell my brain all those logical things. It seems to take a lot more to get into my heart. Like the pastor's-wife thing." Her gaze dropped to the ground. "I know logically I'd be fine, but my heart still finds it scary." She laughed. "Again, ironic, given our current situation, right?"

His mouth went dry. Was she trying to tell him something or was his bias getting in the way again? "If we do get out of here, would you want to figure out that day-to-day stuff together?" The question slipped out before he could filter it.

She twisted to face him and placed her arms around his neck, pulling him close. He wrapped his arms around her waist and steeled himself. He wouldn't repeat the same mistake, as he had earlier in the day. After all, she hadn't answered his question yet. She lifted her face and he felt her cheek brush against his before she whispered in his ear. "Let's fight our way out, like we're back in the boxing ring at the academy. Or die trying."

The door swung open. Joe loosened his grip but before he could turn around, his eyes caught something move, through the window, across the street.

"Sorry to break up the lovely moment." Wyatt was flanked in the doorway by the two men, both of whom had their guns drawn.

Joe didn't fully let go of her as she spun around in his arms. His right hand slid down her arm to her wrist until he gripped her hand. She flashed him a look, but he faced forward, his jaw set. She had tried to make it clear they needed to at least try to fight their way out. In her experience, hand-holding wasn't conducive to self-defense. Was he scared of her timing?

"Well, one of you told the truth. You are Joe Rose," Wyatt said. He turned. "But you are the woman who took down my communications network." His eyes hardened and the polite man in the doorway morphed before her eyes into a cold-blooded leader of a crime ring. "I don't negotiate with people I can't trust."

He wasn't entirely correct, but now wasn't the time. "Then I guess you're not getting your hands on the research," she replied. "Because I made sure it's secure and only accessible if both Joe and I are free."

He stepped into the room and the two men followed, the door closing behind them with a thud. "I don't know what you did to yourself to look like Audrey but you failed to learn about the woman you're pretending to be. Audrey Clark is a woman of science, a woman of integrity. She doesn't have a devious bone in her body."

Oh, how Kendra wanted to reveal that Audrey had actually been the one to bring down Masked's communications network just to see his smug smile drop.

"It's why I invested so much of my time with her all those years ago," he said. "I knew she'd prove valuable someday." He moved closer, scowling at her, but unfortunately not within striking distance. "And if you had done your due diligence on me, you'd know I don't like to change plans. I choose them carefully and make sure we stick to it. So, if you want to live, you either hand over the research now, or you tell me what you did with Audrey, and I'll go back to my initial plan. Your choice."

She didn't need Joe's expertise to know the man was lying through his teeth. He had no intention of letting her live. If he thought she was the one that took down the communications network, the only thing he'd want was revenge. A host of snarky comments jostled in her mind for the right to be said, but Kendra kept her mouth closed.

As she anticipated, this infuriated him more. His eyes flashed with anger. "It seems our guests are choosing option C. Shoot them one body part at a time until I get what I want."

"Kendra." Joe squeezed her hand hard. "It's time to pray."

Wyatt laughed. "That's a new one."

Kendra looked at Joe in disbelief. What about fighting? Her mind flashed back to his story in Afghanistan. Did he know something she didn't? Or did he genuinely want to pray again? He dropped to his knees, and she joined him instantly.

The sound of glass cracking reached her before the first gunman fell back, hit right in the shoulder. The second gunman moved toward Wyatt, presumably to cover him, but another pop sounded and he cried out, hit in the leg. He tripped forward as he fell to the ground but still had the gun. Joe released her hand and elbowed the man in the leg where he'd been shot. He hollered, and Joe twisted and locked himself on the man's arm, fighting to get him to release his gun.

Kendra jumped up into a lunge and, using the momentum, used her other knee to slam into the side of the standing man's leg, aiming for the common peroneal nerve. She knew from experience it would send a shooting pain up and down his spine. He dropped instantly. While he was off balance, she twisted the hand that had a gun in it until he cried out and released it.

Wyatt turned for the door. If he got away, she had a feeling he'd never be seen again.

"Joe!"

"Freeze," Joe yelled at Wyatt. He had also succeeded in getting the gun from the man who was on the ground, hunched over his leg.

Wyatt stooped down, arms over his head, but wrenched the door open, anyway. Joe ran after him and disappeared into the hallway. Kendra jumped up and followed, slamming the door behind her. The keys dangled from the outside of the doorknob. She twisted it to ensure their attackers weren't going anywhere and then ran for the stairs.

Thankfully, having grown up with all brothers, she knew a faster way. She hopped up on the railing and slid down the first flight. Her bones shouted at her that she was getting too old for such antics, but she couldn't let Wyatt get away. She ran across the platform and hopped on the second railing. "Joe, stand aside!"

He moved to the left side without question and she held her right leg out for balance as she slid down and slammed right into Wyatt's back. The impact made her tumble off the railing, but Joe lunged and caught her arm before her head slammed into the cement wall on the other side of the stairs. Joe lifted her fully until she was upright and took the final step, holding down Wyatt.

Approaching footsteps echoed from the stairs below. Joe pointed a gun in the direction of the noise. Around the next landing, a glimpse of the blond hair Kendra had spotted days ago came into view.

"Beverly?" Kendra asked, her voice shaken.

Joe turned back and grinned. "The answer to our prayer."

"Thank you for that," Beverly said, and continued climbing the stairs, a rifle against her back and a Sig Sauer handgun in her grasp. "Was nice to have a clear shot."

Beverly pulled out a pair of handcuffs from her waist. Kendra accepted it and took over for Joe, who wasn't as well-versed in arrest techniques. Wyatt remained silent while she recited his rights and handcuffed him. Joe pulled him upright.

Wyatt's eyes widened at the sight of Beverly. "You?"

"You should've never threatened my daughter." Beverly's voice reverberated with such emotion it caught Kendra off guard.

"We disarmed two men on the tenth," Joe said. He moved to keep his gun aimed at the stairway above, in case others approached.

"They're secure in the room, though they'll need medical attention." Kendra dropped to her knee so she could look into Wyatt's face. "How many other men are here?"

Wyatt turned stone-faced.

"He doesn't like for many to see his face. If there are any more men here, they might not know he's their boss." Beverly grinned. "As soon as I spotted you through that window, I sent an SOS. A task force made up of Homeland Security, FBI and CIA should all be here in a minute to ensure this is done right."

A burst of sound from below confirmed the backup had indeed arrived. DHS agents, hopefully real ones, as well as men and women in FBI jackets rushed forward. Beverly held up a badge. "With the help of the FBI agents Kendra Parker and Joe Rose, the head of the Masked organization is right here."

The next hour seemed to fly by in slow motion. They spent most of the time outside, waiting. An ambulance arrived and offered to take Kendra and Joe, but they both agreed that other than being a little dehydrated they were fine.

Beverly finally approached and the question that had plagued Kendra burst out. "How? The bomb? How are you here?" She didn't even know how to begin.

Her biological mom smiled for the first time. "The bomb was a distraction to give us all time to escape. I had detonators placed on the top floor of that house for ages. I simply set off the south-side ones and everyone came running to check on the men on that side, which gave me ample time to escape on the north side." She pointed at Joe but kept her gaze on Kendra. "As far as being here. I've always believed trust is earned. I placed GPS trackers on all Joe's shoes since I first considered making him an asset. When his signal went cold all of a sudden last night, I knew something was wrong."

"They had us trapped in a building scheduled for demolition and used a cell-phone jammer."

Beverly nodded, as if unsurprised. "He enjoys using jammers when he's scheduled an accident." She held up her fingers in air quotes. "I traveled to where the last ping had been and saw the remains of the building." She seemed to age ten years as she said it before she sighed and all trace of emotion disappeared. "Then I got a moving ping headed to the airport and finally here."

"You found us just in time," Kendra said. "Thank you."

Beverly glanced at Joe. They appeared to have an unspoken language because he cleared his throat. "I'm going to see if anyone needs more from us before we can leave."

"Thank you," Beverly said. She averted her gaze. "When you found me… Well, I couldn't let myself imagine a life where I got to know you as my daughter without putting you in more danger."

Kendra's throat tightened. "And now?"

Beverly frowned, her eyes searching Kendra's face.

"I would like to know both of you. You have no idea how much." Her voice cracked but she pulled back her shoulders. "Bad things tend to follow me around, though, and I couldn't bear it if I hurt you more than I already have."

A knot in Kendra's stomach dissipated. "How about you let us decide if it's worth the risk?"

Beverly's eyes widened before she nodded. "Have you already told your sister?"

Kendra shook her head. "I thought she deserved to hear it from you first, but I'm not going to keep it a secret I met you."

"Thank you. I would like a chance to be in your lives if…" Her face scrunched up. "Well, I'll obviously understand if you don't, but…"

Pain and doubt radiated over Beverly's features with such intensity that Kendra's heart almost burst. Her mom *wanted* to know her. Kendra wasn't ready to hug her, but she desperately looked forward to the day she could. "Yes," she said simply. "I want that, and I'm sure Audrey will, too."

A man in a jacket approached. "Agent Walsh, we're ready for you."

"I'll be there in a minute," Beverly said, studying Kendra's face as if for permission.

"Go." She watched Joe approach. "I'll be fine, but you should know Wyatt arranged for two murders and a drug frame in Audrey's apartment."

Her face hardened again, and the seasoned agent returned. "I'll take care of it. Tell your sister she's free to come home in a couple of days." And with that, Beverly joined the other agents.

Joe placed a hand on Kendra's back. "You have no idea how many reports to a bunch of agencies we'll have to submit."

The paperwork would be atrocious. Necessary, though. She smiled at him. "But not right now. Can I ask you a question?"

"Of course."

"Were you trying to kiss me earlier?" The moment the question was out of her mouth, she regretted her attempt at broaching the subject. He shifted uncomfortably.

"I thought you…" He shrugged. "I don't know what I thought."

"Are there a cluster of cues for when a woman wants a man to kiss her?"

He looked up at the sky. "Well…obviously they can be misread, and every woman is different. In general, there are a set of subtle, unconscious behaviors a woman might display if she's interested or flirting with a man." He rubbed the back of his neck and stared at the ground. "I mean there's the common ones like smiling and making your eyes bigger, but there are also lesser known…"

"For instance…"

He straightened and awkwardly gestured to no one. "Well, activity level can indicate interest. Like a bouncing foot."

Kendra bounced her right heel up and down, the sole of her shoes smacking against the pavement. "Oh?"

He glanced down and laughed. "Not like you're impatient."

"What if I am?" She closed the gap between them.

"Let me be clear. No matter what my behavioral cues may or may not say, I love you."

He exhaled and all signs of nervousness evaporated. The confident man she knew flashed the mischievous smirk she'd missed. "That was about to be my analysis."

"Oh, really?" She was about to playfully argue in response, when his lips brushed against hers, tenderly, and her legs felt weak. She completely forgot her comeback line, but she didn't care.

He placed his hands on her waist and straightened. "I love you, too." Something caught his attention over her shoulder.

Kendra looked to follow his gaze. Beverly crossed her arms over her chest, smiling. "I knew you two would make a good team. You're free to go. I'll be in touch tomorrow."

Kendra turned back to Joe. "Okay. You were right. My mother is a genius."

EPILOGUE

Kendra turned to Joe, admiring how he looked in a charcoal suit with a light blue shirt and silver tie. They made quite the pair as she wore a navy evening gown complete with a silver shoulder wrap. The entire event was decorated like an evening of snow and glitter, perfect for a Christmas wedding. "I've never felt so relaxed in my entire life, which is odd, because I've been wearing heels all day."

They sat on a padded bench in a tiny alcove of the hotel lobby, just taking a quiet moment alone before the reception for Audrey and Lee began.

He placed one arm around her shoulders. "We've had weeks of nonstop debriefing that's finally over. Your sister and Lee have their happily-ever-after. Your families have met and love each other. Your biological mom is retiring from the spy business for good." He touched his fingers, as if checking off boxes. "I think the sentiment makes perfect sense."

She smiled. Her family had doubled in size, as Audrey's parents had basically proclaimed honorary adoption on the spot. "I think Beverly was surprised that proclaiming we were NCS assets only helped a little in the aftermath of paperwork and interviews." Kendra sighed. "I forgot to tell you. Given all the protocols breached, my handler let me know this morning that I'm demoted to the surveillance team for a while."

Joe pulled away from her and tilted his head. "You don't seem too upset."

She grinned. "I'm actually thrilled. It's not behind a desk. Ever since you shared that Proverbs verse with me about trusting and letting Him direct my paths, I'm trying to envision it like an adventure I wouldn't want to pass up." She reached for his hand, hoping he'd understand. "I'm a little nervous, but my head sort of cleared after I got the news. I decided that after my probationary period is over, I'd like to follow my old partner's lead and transfer to recruiting. My handler said the request would likely be approved, as well as his recommendation that I be on call as a crisis-response team leader. It'd be nice to make a difference without having to make arrests." She studied Joe's face for any indication of his thoughts, but he simply smiled. They'd spent every spare moment they had in each other's company or talking on the phone since the incident, but they'd yet to broach the tricky subject of the future. "What about you? Any decisions?" She tried to keep the nerves out of her voice but failed.

"Funny you should mention it." He rubbed his thumb over her palm and placed his other hand on top of hers. "My handler seemed relieved when I turned in my resignation."

"You did it? You're officially going to be a full-time pastor?"

He looked up. "Actually, it turns out that there are a few organizations that need pastors on campuses. I think I'm going to start my quest to be a lifelong student by becoming an adjunct professor. I can handle a small class load, as well as part-time work as a campus pastor. I figure I'll even have margin to volunteer as an FBI chaplain for a crisis team."

She laughed. She couldn't help it. "Oh, is that all?"

He flashed the contagious smirk she loved. "I love variety."

They had that in common. "It does sound kind of perfect for you." She discreetly kicked her heels off underneath her dress and let her toes sink into the carpet. She hated the thought of saying goodbye after the wedding and going their separate ways. "Wouldn't it be funny if we ended up on the same campus and ended up on the same crisis—"

He slipped off the bench, still holding her hands, and dropped to one knee.

The action took her breath away. Her insides shook. Had he dropped something or was he—

"You've just described the mission I've planned. I will end up wherever you're assigned and make that a reality because I love you completely. My intention is to spend the rest of our lives together, if you'll have me. Kendra, will you marry me?"

She sucked in a sharp breath. "Yes," she whispered. She leaned forward and kissed him gently, her hands on either side of his face, until the sound of a DJ announcing that dinner would be served soon reached her ears.

She blinked back the moisture from her eyes. She spotted Audrey's father exiting the reception to wave down a waiter. She gestured for Joe to get up before anyone could see him. "But I want to keep it a secret… just for today." She leaned over and whispered in his ear. "Will you accept this one last covert operation with me?"

He kissed her cheek and beamed. "I wouldn't dream of starting off on the wrong foot with my future sister-in-law. It's Audrey and Lee's day. That's why the ring is still back at my hotel." His face flushed. "I had another proposal planned for the Rose Parade, but I thought my heart was going to burst if I had to wait any longer to ask you."

She kissed him again, overwhelmed yet wanting to jump up and down. Yet, she kept her composure. They walked, hand-in-hand, into the reception area. Audrey caught her eye and practically dragged Lee with her to the back of the room. He narrowly avoided tripping over Audrey's white dress. "I can't believe we're married," Audrey almost shouted, beaming.

Kendra laughed. She realized she couldn't wait to say the same, but her eyes rested on her mom, Audrey's mom and Beverly laughing together at the table behind them. Audrey followed her gaze. "I couldn't have planned a better family reunion." Tears glistened in her eyes, and she reached over to squeeze Kendra's hand. "Thank you for putting up with so much Christmas for me this past week. I know it's not your favorite holiday."

"Oh, I don't know. It's grown on me." Her eyes met Joe's and they shared a knowing look. "A wise man—" Kendra caught herself, realizing it sounded like part of the Christmas story. She reached for her fiancé's hand— she loved thinking of him like that—and leaned into him. "I'm talking about Joe actually. He reminded me that Christmas is really about celebrating the beginning of a successful rescue mission. I can appreciate a holiday that reminds me of that."

Lee chuckled. "Never thought of it that way, but it's a perfect description."

Audrey grinned. "You're beginning to love Christmas."

"I didn't say love—"

Audrey shook her head. "No, I can tell, and it's the best gift you could've given me. We are going to have so much fun next year with all the prep and traditions." Audrey leaned over and embraced Kendra. "By the way, when's the wedding?" she whispered before she straightened.

Kendra gaped, fighting back a laugh. "How did you—"

Audrey rolled her eyes. "Please. I knew it the minute you walked in." Lee grabbed Audrey's hand and began to lead her toward the head table. Audrey looked over her shoulder with a shrug and a wink. "It's a twin thing."

* * * * *

If you enjoyed this story, look for these other books by Heather Woodhaven:

Undercover Twin
Protected Secrets
Tracking Secrets

Dear Reader,

I loved writing Audrey and Kendra so much it's going to be hard to say goodbye. I hope you enjoyed their happy endings as much as I did.

Joe's spiritual realization wasn't planned. I had a different moment in mind for him, but I think it's what we both needed to hear at the time. There is so much freedom that goes with acknowledging and trusting God with every area of your life. The reminder has brought an extra spring to my step.

I may not love all the traditions and preparation for the holidays as much as Audrey, but I do enjoy thinking of Christmas as a time to celebrate a successful rescue mission.

And I'm really craving one of Audrey's gingerbread cookies right about now.

Merry Christmas,
Heather Woodhaven